BLACK BIRD, BLUE ROAD

SOFIYA PASTERNACK

▼ VERSIFY
An Imprint of HarperCollinsPublishers

Versify® is an imprint of HarperCollins Publishers.

Black Bird, Blue Road
Copyright © 2022 by Sofiya Pasternack
All rights reserved. Printed in the United States of America. No part of this
book may be used or reproduced in any manner whatsoever without written
permission except in the case of brief quotations embodied in critical articles
and reviews. For information, address HarperCollins Publishers,
195 Broadway, New York, NY 10007.
www.harpercollinschildrens.com

ISBN 978-0-35-857203-9

Typography by Laura Mock
22 23 24 25 26 PC/LSCC 10 9 8 7 6 5 4 3 2 1

First Edition

To C and C—

I would poke an angel in the eyes for you.

PART ONE

Hello!

Come in.

Sit down.

Don't be scared. This is a very important story, after all, and you shouldn't be afraid to hear it. It's from a very long time ago. A thousand years! In those days, they used to begin their stories like this: *There was one, there was no one.* So that's how I'll begin, too.

There was one. A girl. Ziva bat Leah, the daughter of a judge and the sister of a prophet.

There was no one. No one to believe that Ziva could do the things she set out to do—like find a cure for her brother's illness, or master a demon, or sway the Angel of Death, whom she called *malach ha-mavet.*

Ziva did two of those things, dear listener.

Which two?

Well.

There was one, there was no one. And on the shores of Bahr ul-Khazar, which you call the Caspian Sea, Ziva bat Leah, who didn't know yet about a cure or a demon or *malach ha-mavet,* woke up on her twelfth birthday in the city of Atil, and her first thought was—

ONE

I HAVE TO CUT OFF Pesah's finger today.

Ziva lay on the floor of her twin brother's room, staring at the ceiling. She listened to the wet, thick breaths of Pesah in his bed above her, letting out her own quiet sigh of relief at the sound of his breathing. Even if his breathing did sound terrible, and had sounded that way for weeks. She didn't want to get up, but she needed to do so before anyone went to her room to check on her.

So she got up as quietly as she could so she didn't wake him, folding up the thin sheet and shoving it under Pesah's bed along with the thin straw mattress, and thought about things. About turning twelve years old. That meant she was responsible for herself. No longer were her parents accountable if Ziva broke a law or infracted a rule.

Like the rule against sleeping in Pesah's room with him. Baba's brother, Uncle Sabriel, was a doctor in Samkarsh, and when Pesah had gotten sick, Uncle Sabriel started to make the trip to Atil every few months to see him. The previous spring, he had recommended that Pesah be moved out of the room he shared with Ziva and into private quarters. Pesah's illness could spread, Uncle Sabriel said. But Ziva and Pesah had been in the same room for two years while Pesah had been sick, and Ziva hadn't developed any of the lesions or white patches that covered Pesah's body. Even though she pointed this out to everyone, they moved Pesah into the room next to hers. They were apart, but they still slept against the same wall, and would tap back and forth to one another as they fell asleep.

Then this spring, Uncle Sabriel had said Pesah should be moved to his own separate building. So, one of the gardens was replanted elsewhere and the land was used for a new building for Pesah to live in. That had been too much. Too far away. No matter how much Ziva tapped on the wall, Pesah wouldn't be able to tap back. So she started sneaking to his house after dark, setting up a bed on the floor.

If she got caught now, even though she was certain she was immune to whatever was making Pesah ill, would she get in even more trouble?

Well, she was also responsible for unwrapping all his careful bandages and looking at how his disease was slowly eating him away. And she was accountable for amputating his fingers and toes as they succumbed to his illness. There were servants who should have been caring for him, but they didn't do it right. So Ziva did it. That deserved some kind of concession. Right?

Before she left, Ziva grabbed her favorite brooch from the table beside Pesah's bed, where she'd put it the night before. Her mother had gotten it for her, even though Ziva was sure it had just been because her mother thought it was pretty, and not because she recognized its greater significance. It was an iron date palm tree with four purple gems clustered where the dates would grow on a real tree. Since the moment she'd gotten it, the brooch hadn't left Ziva's immediate area.

Palm brooch in one hand, Ziva opened Pesah's door and peered out into the gray morning garden, watching for anyone to catch her exiting Pesah's house. No one was around, so she slipped out and hurried to the main house, back to her room. Inside, she observed the messed-up bedsheets she'd arranged the night before, then made the bed haphazardly. A bat mitzvah was responsible for making her own bed, right?

Yes. There'd be a list of new responsibilities for her once her parents found her. Worst of all, now she'd be expected to entertain courting from boys in the city, like Reuven ben Kohen. She stuck her tongue out at the wrinkled sheets atop her bed. *Yuck.*

Pesah still had another year. Even though he was twelve, too. It took boys extra time to grow up, Ziva supposed.

The door opened and she whirled toward it. Setareh, her mother's maid, poked her head into the room and sang softly, *"Tavalodet mobarak!"*

Setareh was from Persia, south of the Khazar Sea, and Ziva knew enough Persian to know what Setareh was saying: *Happy birthday!*

"Thank you, Setareh." Ziva said, heart thumping. If she'd returned five minutes later, Setareh would have caught her sneaking back in.

"Hurry and get dressed," Setareh said. "Your mother has a wonderful gift prepared for you."

Ziva hesitated. Her mother. "Does she have a wonderful gift prepared for Pesah, too?"

Setareh sighed through her nose at Ziva, and that was answer enough.

Setareh left, and Ziva hurried to her wardrobe. She swapped her nightdress for her favorite red-and-cream kaftan with bronze buttons carved like flowers, pinning her palm brooch to the chest. She combed out and braided her long, dark hair, fastening it at the end with a red ribbon. Her mother had bought her the latest hair baubles from Byzantium—combs with jewels and carved ivory figurines affixed to the top— but Ziva had put them in a drawer and never worn them. She wasn't a Byzantine girl. She was a Khazar, and in Khazaria, girls didn't put fancy combs into their hair.

As she checked herself over, she reflected that in Khazaria, girls also didn't cut off their brothers' fingers.

Well, she wouldn't for much longer, because she and Pesah were going to find a cure soon. Her brilliant brother would come up with a remedy for his disease, cure himself, and then cure everyone else with it, too. She could feel it in her bones.

TWO

ON HER WAY TO PESAH'S HOUSE, Ziva did a lap around the front courtyard, looking for any pebbles that would make good skipping stones. Before Pesah's illness had taken the use of his hands, they'd spent hours skipping stones on the river. They would again, Ziva knew, and she was going to be prepared for that day.

There! She snatched one up, inspecting its smooth, flat surface. It was perfect. She brushed some dust off it before dropping it in her pocket, and as it settled against her leg, someone walked into the courtyard. A messenger, from the look of him. He was road-weary and dirty, and when he saw Ziva, he let out a sigh of relief and approached her.

He bowed. "Good morning. Are you a lady of this house?"

Ziva returned his bow and hesitated a moment. "I am."

He opened the satchel at his side and handed her a scroll. "A letter from Samkarsh."

She brightened. Uncle Sabriel was the only person she knew who lived in Samkarsh, and she grinned as she took the letter from the messenger. He'd probably written to send birthday wishes to Ziva and Pesah, and to announce his yearly holiday visit. She unrolled it before she thought to pay the messenger, even, and was about to look up from the scroll and apologize when her eyes touched upon a sentence that shocked the smile off her face:

—best course of action is to move Pesah out of Atil and to Samkarsh immediately—

Ziva gaped at that fragment of words, too shocked to even read the next line, until the messenger cleared his throat. She looked up at him, mouth hanging open with surprise, and then realized.

"Oh." She rummaged in her pockets for any money to give him. Uncle Sabriel would have paid him the bulk of the delivery cost, but it was expected to give him something for getting the letter to them safely. She found a little bit and handed it to him. "Sorry. Here. Thank you."

The messenger took the money, thanked her, and left. Ziva stood alone in the courtyard with the opened scroll clutched in her fingers.

Move Pesah out of Atil.

Move Pesah out of Atil?

To Samkarsh, all the way on the other side of the khaganate.

She opened the scroll again.

She read the rest of the sentence:

In light of our previous conversations about Pesah's worsening health, I now believe the best course of action is to move Pesah out of Atil and to Samkarsh immediately, a transition I can accomplish myself when I come for Rosh Hashanah.

Ziva let her arms drop, the scroll half-rolled in her hands. They wanted to take Pesah away from her because he was getting sicker. But then, why weren't they working harder to find a cure for him?

She shook her head as she rolled the scroll up tightly. No. They wouldn't take Pesah. She wouldn't let them. She'd find a cure by then, and everyone would see that Pesah was fine, and he would stay in Atil with Ziva. Ziva darted inside the house and handed the newly rolled-up scroll to the first servant she came across, and then walked as fast as she could to Pesah's house.

Pesah had gotten up while Ziva was gone and was sitting at his window. When he saw Ziva, he brightened and waved. She waved back, deciding not to tell him about the letter, and when she got into his house she stooped to hug him in his chair and said, "Happy, happy birthday."

"Happy birthday, birthday," he said back to her, doing his best to wrap his arms around her. His voice, muffled by the bandages that wrapped around his face, sounded wet. He coughed as he pulled away from Ziva. The cough was wet, too.

He'd had that cough for way too long.

Ziva kept her frown to herself. "Look what I found." She showed him the pebble.

"That's a good one," Pesah said.

Ziva crossed to his biggest bookshelf and set the stone in an empty spot. The shelves were littered with stones between books and journals and other bookshelf things. "For when you're better." She patted the shelf.

Pesah smiled at her. "You're going to run out of shelf space soon."

Ziva shrugged. "We've got a lot of stone skipping to make up for, you know. Close the window so I can look at your skin."

Pesah said, "I'm fine, Ziva." He said that every time, but this time he added, "Plus, Irbis just left. He put new bandages on."

Ziva frowned as she pulled the gauzy curtains over the windows, obscuring Pesah from anyone who might be near his house, but leaving enough light to see by. "Which bandages?"

"My arms," Pesah said, lifting them up to demonstrate.

"It would make me feel better to check myself," Ziva said, knowing Irbis did what her parents told him to do, but there was no way he could take care of Pesah better than Ziva could.

Pesah laughed. "Yes, Doctor."

Ziva pretend-scowled at him. "You know I don't want to be a doctor. That's what *you're* going to do."

"Well, a judge wouldn't dress someone's wounds," Pesah said. "So I can't say, 'Yes, Your Honor.'"

Ziva shrugged. "I mean. You *can*."

Pesah laughed, and Ziva went to the makeshift laboratory that she and Pesah had put together in the spring. They were working on salves that might help Pesah's illness, but two weeks ago Ziva hadn't been paying attention and Pesah had burned his finger. He hadn't even felt it. Irbis had changed Pesah's bandages, sure, but he didn't know about the burn. He didn't know that when Pesah got any kind of wound, it was only a matter of time before it turned dark.

At the laboratory, Ziva reached for a smallish bucket. Inside were a pair of very sharp, shining shears. They were from Uncle Sabriel, who had shown Baba how to use them to amputate Pesah's infected fingers and toes. Ziva had watched, too, lingering in the doorway. And now that Uncle Sabriel had gone back to Samkarsh, and Baba couldn't stomach the blood, and Ziva's mother acted like Pesah was already a ghost, the responsibility of Pesah's amputations fell to Ziva.

The linen cabinet was filled with stacks of clean gauze, and Ziva fetched enough of those to cover Pesah's arms, legs, and face. She had just done his chest yesterday, and his chest was never as bad as the rest of him.

Ziva pulled a stool in front of Pesah and started with his feet and legs. The disease twisted his bones, bending his ankles and swelling his feet so he couldn't hold his own weight anymore. When Uncle Sabriel found out, he brought a wicker chair with wheels on the bottom so Pesah could be pushed around with ease. It allowed Ziva to take Pesah around the property and through the gardens, even though he always said he was fine in his room.

Pesah didn't look at what Ziva was doing. A medical pamphlet from Byzantium—a gift from Uncle Sabriel—sat on his lap, and he read it while Ziva inspected him. She glanced at the pamphlet once and snorted. It was in Greek, and even though Ziva could write her name out in Greek, she couldn't make sense of the language. Pesah could, plus Latin. And he was good at mathematics, able to do big equations in his head. He had memorized every book in the house. When he could still use his hands, he'd drawn schematics for fabulous but silly inventions, like a lever on a wagon that could stop the wheels from turning, or a machine that spun clothes around to dry them after they were washed. They were still in his room, tucked away on some bookshelf somewhere. It worried her that he never pulled the books down to look at his old sketches, even when Ziva offered to do it for him. She thought she knew why. Even the sage, level-tempered Pesah got sad when he was reminded of the things he couldn't do anymore.

That would change when they figured out a cure. She knew it. He'd be sketching new, ridiculous inventions in no time.

Ziva discarded the old gauze in the bucket and inspected the lesions on his feet and legs. His skin was discolored by darker patches that surrounded raised flesh-colored or whitish lumps. She used a gauze-wrapped finger to poke one firmly.

Pesah didn't act like he'd felt her touch him at all.

"Pesah," Ziva said.

He looked down at her. "Hm?"

"Does that hurt?"

"Does what hurt?" Then he looked at where she pressed on one of the lumps, blinked, and said, "I don't feel anything."

"That's good, I guess," Ziva said softly. He had these same lumps on his face, hands, and feet, even worse than they were on his arms, legs, and chest. They looked terrible, but at least they didn't hurt.

That day, mercifully, his feet and legs looked no worse. No new lumps, darker discoloration, or infection that Ziva could see. She wrapped Pesah's legs and feet back up in fresh gauze.

"Listen to this, Ziva," Pesah said, nodding at the pamphlet on his lap. "Alchemists in the north have developed a salve that's supposed to keep wounds from darkening."

Ziva perked, her mind jumping to Uncle Sabriel's letter. "A cure?"

Pesah shrugged. "Maybe? There's a recipe here, but the notes say—"

His words were eaten by a wet, racking cough. He turned his head away from Ziva as his entire body coughed, pushing out whatever was inside his lungs. Ziva stood, rubbing him softly on the back, wishing she could do something—anything—for him.

He coughed out one final, choking sound, gasping in wet and rasping breaths, then said, "Sorry." He cleared the wetness from his throat and said, "Um, the notes say it's imperfect. But it's a start!"

Ziva returned to her stool. "Yeah," she said. "It's a start."

She unwrapped his arms and hands.

His arms were much like his legs: splotchy, discolored, covered with lumps and bumps. His hands made Ziva want to scream with frustration. Four of his fingers were already gone, collected by infection, and a fifth, the middle finger of his left hand, was swollen and shiny, and the wicked red color it had been was turning dark, like a bruise.

It smelled like the other fingers had. Uncle Sabriel said when a wound smelled like that, and started to turn black, there was only one thing to do. Something Irbis and the other servants wouldn't do. So Ziva had to.

"What's the recipe call for?" Ziva asked as she picked up the shears. She had to keep talking, had to keep thinking about something other than what she was about to do. This would be the third of his fingers that she'd cut off—Uncle Sabriel had done the first two—but her hands would still tremble if she thought too much about it.

Pesah went back to reading his pamphlet. "The recipe calls for . . . spear-leek, which, I'm not sure what that is. And crop-leek. I don't know what that is either. Two kinds of leeks. We can ask at the market."

Ziva held his infected finger out straight, away from his other fingers, and slipped the shears' blades a tiny way down from where the blackness ended, like Uncle Sabriel had instructed. She didn't want to cut his finger off and leave some of the infection by accident. He'd lose this finger just above the second knuckle, which wasn't as bad as one of the others. That one had been cut all the way down to the webbing between fingers.

She felt eyes on her, and when she looked up, Pesah's blue gaze was fixed on her. Did he look worried? Frightened? Apprehensive?

The bandages on his face shifted up and his eyes crinkled around the edges. He was smiling.

Of course he was smiling. Pesah knew what needed to be done. Someone with less knowledge about infection would beg to keep their fingers, but Pesah understood better than Ziva did what it would mean to leave the finger there.

"Don't worry, Ziva," he said, and his reassurance gave her the strength she needed to pull the handles of the shears together swiftly, smoothly. The infected finger dropped into the bucket and was lost in the gauze there. Pesah didn't so much as flinch. "We'll figure something out."

THREE

ZIVA WRAPPED PESAH'S AMPUTATED FINGER in linen to stop the bleeding, then applied protective gauze over his arms and hands.

As Ziva got him dressed, Pesah continued to read the pamphlet from Byzantium. "Wine. Yep. Bull's gall. I bet we can get some from the butcher. It has to be left in a brass bowl for nine days. Do we have a brass bowl?"

"Mother has one," Ziva said.

"Can we use it?" Pesah asked.

"We can if she doesn't notice it's missing," Ziva said.

Pesah laughed under the bandages over his face. "She'll be so mad."

Ziva looked at the finger in the bucket, wondering if the salve would help Pesah grow back all the things that she'd cut off him.

She looked up at him, needing to take her eyes away from the dead finger in the bucket. Pesah noticed and met her gaze. His face was bandaged so much, all she could make out were his blue eyes, untouched by the disease so far. The bandages were there to keep the lesions across his cheeks and chin clean, and to cover up his missing nose, his scarred skin, his scourged lips. Pesah's nervous habit was to chew on his lips, and when he could still feel them, it had been a gentle nibbling. But when the disease numbed his face along with his hands and feet, he'd started to bite too hard. He couldn't feel when he chewed his lip to pulp.

"Whatever she's using the bowl for isn't as important as finding a cure for you," Ziva said.

Pesah laughed and said, "I guess."

Ziva got him dressed in a celestial kaftan that made his blue eyes blaze. The kaftan was embroidered with red, a patterned border of birds in flight. His trousers hung loose because boots hurt his feet, and Ziva hadn't yet figured out how to tuck trousers into soft slippers. She affixed his kippah to his thick brown hair; the kippah was red, like her brow band and braid ribbon were red, to mark their ancestral lineage from the steppe.

When Pesah was distracted by choosing a book to bring outside, Ziva reached into the bucket and plucked the amputated finger out. She wrapped it up in gauze and tucked it into her pocket.

She pushed Pesah in his chair outside, toward the orchard with all the apple trees in it. It was still early enough that it wasn't boiling hot, like it would be later that day, but Ziva still parked Pesah in the deep shade of a large apple tree to keep the heat away.

She sat on the ground next to him, kicking her legs out from under her kaftan. She inspected a couple of pebbles for skipping suitability and added one to her pocket, then let herself flop back onto the grass, knowing her mother would tut endlessly at her if she was caught.

"I'll go to the market later," Ziva said. "For spear-leek and . . . what's the other thing?"

"Crop-leek," Pesah said, voice soft. He coughed again, but it wasn't as bad this time. "And bull's gall."

"Is bull's gall kosher?" Ziva asked, staring at the sky through the apple tree's leafy canopy.

Pesah shrugged. "I don't know. It's a recipe from the north. The Geats? I don't think they keep kosher. It might not be."

Ziva caught herself chewing on her bottom lip and stopped. If Pesah couldn't do it, she wouldn't either. "Bulls are kosher animals. As long as the slaughter is kosher, taking its gall should be fine." She hesitated. "Right?"

He didn't answer. The two of them sat in their separate thoughts for a while. Ziva mostly felt that awareness of the severed finger in her pocket, and she thought about going out to the family burial plot, putting it in the secret hole she'd dug with the other four she'd cut off him. She glanced at her brother. He stared at the garden wall, the gate, the sky beyond. His kaftan, celestial blue, like his eyes, like the sky—but then

Ziva imagined him all in white, what was left of him, interred in the earth, missing so many pieces. Her beautiful brother. Taken.

No.

She wasn't going to let that happen.

She'd get what he needed from the market and they could start working on the salve from Geatland that day.

A pair of servants crossed the orchard from the other side, cutting through as they went from one side of the property to the other. Ziva saw them. Pesah saw them. Then they saw Pesah. And they stopped, lingered a moment, and hurried in a different direction.

Ziva got to her feet, ready to yell for them to come back so she could chastise them. She'd barely gathered the breath she needed to yell when Pesah's soft voice stopped her.

"It's Rosh Chodesh Elul," he said.

She held her anger in check when she said, "I know."

"So . . ." Pesah glanced at the fleeing servants. "How can we be kinder people in the next year than we were this year?"

She blew out her anger and hurt in a long, slow, exasperated breath. "Not yell at servants."

"That's a good start."

Ziva pointed a stiff finger at them. "They're being disrespectful."

"It's okay," Pesah said, wincing a little. He rubbed his forehead with a finger. "I understand why they went away."

Ziva understood, but she still didn't like it. She jammed her fists onto her hips and said simply, "Hmph."

"Let's go inside," Pesah mumbled. "I have a headache. The sun is making it worse."

She glanced after the fleeing servants, then back to Pesah. "Okay."

Ziva took him back. The medical pamphlet was limp in his fingers. Some of the brightness was gone from his eyes. In the private coolness of his house, he said, "I'm kind of tired today. I'm going to rest."

Ziva nodded, helping him into bed as she said, "I'll go to the market to get some leeks, and . . ."

"Bull's gall," Pesah said with a smile.

"Bull's gall," Ziva whispered to herself so she'd remember. "Yeah. And we'll start making the salve when I get back."

"You don't have to do that today," Pesah said. "It's our birthday. Mama's probably got something planned. You should enjoy it."

"I don't care about birthdays, or whatever she's got planned," Ziva said. "I care about *you*, Pesah."

He laughed softly. "One day isn't going to make a difference."

"What if it does?" Ziva pressed, thinking of how close Rosh Hashanah really was, and Pesah sighed.

"Okay," he said, and as Ziva left, she resolved to not let Pesah touch any of the instruments that could hurt him.

FOUR

BEFORE SHE COULD GO to the market, Ziva had to bury Pesah's finger.

Her family estate had a small burial plot on it. Ziva's father, Mänäs, was a judge on the highest court of Atil, as his father had been before him, and his father, and so on. Her family had owned this land for five generations. Before that, they'd lived on the steppe. Now they lived in Atil, the capital, away from their ancestral grazing lands. But Ziva was fine with living in the city, and fine only having a passing familiarity with horses and caravans and archery. Pesah never would have survived on the steppe.

The burial plot held the simple graves of Ziva's forebears, with simple stone markers bearing their names. She walked past Benyamin and Aharon, her grandfather and great uncle. Khatun, Benyamin's wife. Khatir and Parsbit, their father and mother. Mänäs, her great-grandfather, for whom her father was named. And Rivka, Mänäs's mother, the family's first landowner.

Behind Rivka's marker, Ziva disturbed the bare spot in the grass. She dug there often. Four fingers were under the dirt in varying stages of decay, all wrapped in linen. She didn't inspect them, just placed the newest finger alongside the others and smoothed the dirt back over them.

Ziva stood and surveyed the graves. How long before Pesah joined them? Where would his grave be? How much of him would there be left to bury?

The last thought made Ziva's lip tremble, and she stiffened it.

No.

Pesah wasn't going to die.

He could figure out the cure somehow, and she'd be there to help him. If he lost all his fingers in the process, she'd work until she lost her own.

"Ziva!"

Her mother's singsong voice chirped through the graveyard. Ziva shut her eyes and sighed.

"Yes, Mother?" she said.

Ziva's mother didn't wear kaftans. She'd been taken with Byzantine fashion, so when she swept past the graves it was in a long red dress with a pink shawl draped across her shoulders. Both the dress and the shawl were patterned with repeating circles of blue and green. The colors were so garish they made Ziva wince.

Setareh trailed behind her, dressed in a kaftan like a proper Khazar.

Ziva's mother plucked at her kaftan, brushing something off the shoulder. "Happy birthday, my sweet girl."

"Thank you," Ziva said softly.

"Twelve years old!" Ziva's mother sighed wistfully. "I remember when I turned twelve years old. My parents threw me a marvelous party! I met your father that night. He was too shy to speak to me. Isn't that funny?"

Ziva didn't think so. Her father was very soft-spoken and didn't enjoy big parties. He was more interested in working: defining and defending the laws of the empire.

Ziva's mother continued on: "Of course, he didn't ask me to marry him that night. How silly that would have been! But our parents began to speak, and a few years later . . ." She shrugged and smiled brightly, then smoothed down Ziva's hair. "I have a surprise for your birthday, Ziva!"

Ziva thought she knew what it was, but she mustered up a scrap of hope and said, "I can spend the day in the law books with Baba?"

"Of course not, silly!" Ziva's mother said. "It's a big party tonight! With all your friends! And maybe you'll meet your destiny just like I did." She winked at Ziva, like they shared a secret.

Ziva smiled, but it felt like a grimace. She didn't want to have a party. She didn't have time to waste on finding her destiny, her soul mate. She needed to get to the market and find the things Pesah needed, and now she had to do all that and get back before Pesah was too busy at the party to . . .

Pesah. At the party.

Ziva blurted out, "Does Pesah get a birthday party?"

Setareh cleared her throat, but Ziva ignored her. Ziva's mother's face lost some of its radiance.

"Of course he does," she said. "But that will be just the family. He doesn't like crowds."

Normally, Ziva would have held her tongue. But today, maybe because she was twelve now and responsible, she instead let her words come rushing out. "Yes he does. He does like crowds. He likes them way more than I do. I hate parties and crowds and I don't have any friends."

"Ziva," her mother said, face red. She sounded breathless and alarmed. "Of course you have friends."

"No, I don't," Ziva said. "And I don't care. I can have friends later. When Pesah isn't sick anymore."

"Ziva—"

"Pesah loves parties and it would probably make him feel a lot better if you let him go to some," Ziva said. "But you won't. You don't let him see any people because he's ugly now."

"Ziva!" her mother gasped. "What a terrible thing to say!"

"It's the truth!" Ziva replied.

Her mother didn't say anything else. She just gaped at Ziva with her hand at her throat, eyes sparkling with tears. Setareh looked profoundly disappointed behind her. Ziva knew she should feel ashamed or sorry for her outburst, but she didn't. It felt good to yell at someone about how unfairly Pesah was treated. Even if that someone was her own mother.

"I have to get to the market before it closes," Ziva said, and she ran out of the burial yard before her mother or Setareh could say anything to stop her.

FIVE

IT WAS SUMMER, so the city's Khazar neighborhoods were mostly empty, the houses shut against the season's heat. A few months prior, when the warming days melted the snow off rooftops and stone streets, the Khazars had packed up their wagons and families. They'd taken their flocks and herds that had wintered on the sea's shores and returned to the steppe. When the Khazars had all been nomads, they had called themselves by colors based on where their livestock grazed.

They still did, in a way.

Ziva's family lived halfway up the hill that made up the central fortress of the city of Atil, and as she let the hill pull her down toward the Volga River where the market was, she took note of the people who had returned from the steppe early. The wagons were always painted with their ancestral colors: bright reds, deep blacks, glaring whites. Ziva's family had an old red wagon they didn't use anymore, and her red brow band marked her as a Red Khazar, at home on the southern steppe. The White Khazars grazed to the west, by the white fortress Sarkel, but not as far as Kyiv. The Black Khazars were northerners, bordering the Bulghars of the Volga. East, the Celestial Khazars. The Blue ones, the ones who still called themselves Asena. The ones who, fireside stories said, could change into wolves.

In the spring and at the end of the summer, there were never wagons painted blue. The Celestial Khazars stayed on the steppe.

As Ziva approached the market, even though it was half as large as it would be in the autumn when the Khazar wagons returned, the mixing and the openness of Atil became more and more apparent. People of every nation, selling and buying. Ships and rafts swarmed on the river, thick as flies on cattle, vying for a dock to tie to. Flags bearing symbols of foreign kings, the delicious smells of exotic foods, the chatter of languages as far away as seas to the east or the west.

Before Pesah's disease had taken his ability to walk, he and Ziva had come to the market. He loved the chaos of the market and all the different people he could talk to about a thousand different things. He practiced Greek and Latin here, and had learned greetings in a dozen other languages. But as his disease got worse, he'd stopped talking to people. And then he'd stopped going.

Ziva plunged into the crowd, shaking away her sadness. Pesah would come here again one day. She just needed to figure out what spear-leek and crop-leek were.

The market was organized, but only if someone understood the laws of kashrut. One side of the market was kosher; the other side was not. The Muslim inhabitants of the city grasped this organizational system faster than the Christians. The Tengrists thought kashrut was odd, but they didn't complain. The Zoroastrians liked it, because even though they didn't follow kashrut exactly, they required their animals to be killed mercifully, and they trusted the kosher butchers to do that. They also knew that the kosher butchers knew exactly which animal the meat had came from. The Zoroastrians didn't eat cattle.

Ziva headed to the kosher side. She was more familiar with the merchants over there. She wandered between the produce booths, inspecting the merchandise for anything she didn't recognize that could be her two types of leek. She asked the merchants about spear-leek and crop-leek, but none of them knew what they were. She bought regular leek, just in case, and some onions. Because their stems sort of looked like spears, didn't they?

Bull's gall now. Ziva was headed toward where the butchers would be, to go to the one Baba liked best and see how much he'd charge for bull's gall, when someone said her name from behind her.

She recognized that voice.

She thought about not turning around, about ignoring the person, but she knew he'd just follow her around the market. So she turned. Reuven ben Kohen was approaching from up the street, waving. His kaftan and kippah were black, like his father's always were. He wasn't alone. His younger brother Shmuel and his friend Yitzhak were with him. When the trio drew closer to Ziva, all three boys put their hands on their chests and bowed a little as a greeting. Then Shmuel and Yitzhak lingered behind Reuven.

"Good afternoon, Ziva bat Leah," Reuven said. He smiled wide. He was a Black Khazar, and a lot of Black Khazars had aquamarine eyes and red hair—even though, in Ziva's opinion, it made more sense for the Red Khazars to have red hair. Obviously. Reuven's hair was only tinted red when the sun hit it just right, and brown otherwise, but he had gotten the aquamarine eyes of the Black Khazars. He was handsome, Ziva supposed, if she was supposed to notice that kind of thing now.

But she still didn't like him.

"Hello, Reuven," Ziva said with as little enthusiasm as possible. Reuven was a year older than Ziva, and was their rabbi's son, so she saw him way more often than she would have liked. He had once played with Pesah in the synagogue's garden after services, but now he wouldn't even acknowledge Pesah's existence.

Reuven fidgeted, then glanced up at the sky. "Nice day."

"Mm-hm." Ziva was done wasting her time. She turned toward the butcher and started walking again.

"Wait!" Reuven darted to her side. "I just, um . . . I never get to talk to you, that's all."

"You know where I live," Ziva said.

He paused for a long time. "I do."

Ziva didn't say anything else. She just seethed under her skin. She knew why Reuven didn't come visit their home. Pesah. It was beyond Ziva's comprehension how Reuven could forsake Pesah the way he had, when the boys had been such close friends when they were younger.

They were almost to the butcher when Reuven pointed to the leeks and onions in Ziva's fist. "Did you come here shopping? Don't you have servants for that?"

Ziva snorted. "I needed some things right now. I didn't want to wait for someone else to do the shopping."

"What other things?" Reuven asked.

"Bull's gall."

His face scrunched with confusion. "What?"

"Bull's," Ziva said, slower, "gall."

"Why?"

Ziva almost told him it was none of his business, but she managed to hold her tongue. They had reached the butcher, another Shmuel like Reuven's brother, and he leaned over the counter and crossed his big arms as he smiled. "Well, good afternoon, little judge."

Ziva liked the butcher a lot. He knew Baba, and he knew Ziva wanted to be a judge like Baba. And Shmuel the butcher, unlike others around the city, didn't laugh at that idea.

"I'd like some bull's gall, please," Ziva said.

One of the butcher's thick eyebrows lifted up. He said, "How much?"

Ziva didn't know. Pesah hadn't specified. "I guess the full amount you'd get from a single bull."

He nodded and told her the price, and went to wrap up the gall while Ziva dug coins out of her pocket. While she did, Reuven shifted beside her.

"Is this . . . for dinner?" he asked.

"No." Ziva set her coins out on the counter for the butcher. "It's medicine."

She expected him to ask what for, but he didn't. She looked at him in time to see him rolling his eyes.

Rage flared hot behind her eyes and she barked, "What was that look for?"

"What look?" He held his hands up. "I didn't make a look."

"You did so!" Ziva said. "You rolled your eyes."

"I . . ." He pressed his lips together. "I just think maybe making medicine isn't something you should be spending your time on."

She jammed her hands onto her hips. "Is that right? What *should* I be doing, then?"

"Oh, come on, Ziva." Reuven glanced back at Shmuel and Yitzhak, and then sighed. "You're a bat mitzvah now. You should be doing stuff that's going to be good for your future family."

She lowered her chin, fixing him with the most ferocious glare she could muster. "My future family is going to benefit from me being a great judge in Atil. *And*, thanks to this medicine, they're going to benefit from having Pesah as a wonderful uncle."

Reuven's upper lip curled at Pesah's name. "No medicine can cure him."

"What do *you* know?" Ziva snapped.

"I know he's dying!" Reuven snapped back. "And I know girls aren't judges!"

"Then you're more stupid than you look!" Ziva grabbed her palm brooch and pulled it away from her kaftan, right at his face. "You're the rabbi's son and you don't even know about Devorah the Prophetess! The fourth judge of Israel!"

"I know about Devorah," Reuven said, glaring at the brooch.

Ziva returned the brooch to her chest, the fury at Reuven making her head feel tight and hot. "Then you should know girls can be judges. And you should get it into your empty head that Pesah *isn't* dying."

Before Reuven could say anything else, Shmuel the butcher was back with a paper-wrapped package. "Here's that gall, little judge." He collected the coins from the counter with a big hand and set the package down with the other.

Ziva snatched up the package, still trembling with rage at Reuven. "Thank you."

"Of course," he said. "Give your father and mother my best wishes."

"I will," Ziva said, and turned away from Reuven. Without another word to him, she marched away from the market, and he didn't follow.

SIX

BEFORE ZIVA COULD GO BACK to Pesah's house, she had to get the other pieces of the recipe: wine and a brass bowl. There was plenty of wine in the kitchens, and as long as Ziva was sneaky, she'd be able to snatch some without an issue.

The real problem would be the brass bowl.

Ziva's mother loved her *things*.

But Ziva knew her mother used her bowls for holding stupid things, like jewelry and perfume and kohl mixtures for her eyes. And none of that was as important as Pesah. Plus, she could use any old bowl to hold jewelry. They specifically needed a brass bowl for the recipe.

Ziva went to the kitchen first and grabbed a ceramic bowl from there. Maybe if she put her mother's things inside a different bowl, she wouldn't realize Ziva had taken the brass one.

It was the middle of the day, so her mother should be outside somewhere complaining about how hot it was. Ziva hurried to the part of the house where her parents' bedroom and bath suite were. She and Pesah had never been allowed into the bedroom, and when they were occasionally summoned there to get a lecture, it always felt so much more serious.

Ziva padded down the hallway, alert for servants. At the heavy door with brass nails along the outside, Ziva paused and listened. When she didn't hear anything to betray her mother's presence inside the room, she eased the door open and peered inside.

The room was enormous in comparison to Ziva's, the stone floors made warm and soft by a gigantic, thick, woven carpet from Khorasan. Her parents' sprawling bed sat on top of the carpet, made up smartly by their servants. Gauzy curtains hung around it from the ceiling, terribly mismatched with the rest of the room. Ziva's mother said that bed curtains were what all the noble ladies in Constantinople had.

Ziva hurried in, feeling like a trespassing thief, and crossed the room to her mother's vanity near the wardrobe that held all her colorful Byzantine gowns. She spotted several metal bowls full of various things, and it was at that moment she realized she wasn't entirely sure what the difference was between brass and copper.

While she stood there, staring at the metal bowls on her mother's vanity with a growing sense of dread, she heard a sour little voice inside her head which pointed out that

Pesah probably knew the difference between brass and copper, and if he were here, he'd already have picked the correct bowl and gone.

Then, another voice.

"I don't like being pulled out of the garden, Mänäs."

Her mother.

And, Mänäs. That was Baba's name.

Ziva panicked and froze. The voices were out in the hallway, coming closer, and Ziva knew at any moment they'd come inside and catch her poking around somewhere she definitely wasn't supposed to be. She ducked into her mother's expansive wardrobe as the door to the room opened and her parents came in.

The door shut with a heavy *thump*. Baba said, "Leah, this is important."

Ziva's mother scoffed. *"Everything* is *always* important."

A pause while Baba took a deep breath. "Sabriel sent a letter," Baba said. "He'll be here for the High Holidays, and he wants Pesah to go with him back to Samkarsh afterward."

Ziva's chest froze, her breath stagnating in her mouth. Baba had gotten the letter, then. Her mother sucked in a gasp outside the wardrobe.

"Why?" she asked. "Samkarsh? Is there treatment there?"

Baba was quiet for a while. He was a slow and measured responder most of the time. He'd told Ziva that, in court, it wasn't wise for a judge to respond right away, without at least repeating the question in his mind. So Baba would wait, consider his thoughts, and then speak them. He was doing that now, letting his thoughts settle before speaking.

Ziva knew from experience that the longer Baba's pauses were, the more serious his thoughts were.

He was silent for what felt like an eternity.

"I don't know," Baba said. "There might be. In any case, I think we should allow Sabriel to take him."

When Ziva's mother spoke, she sounded on the verge of tears. "Oh, Mänäs, let our little boy go live in a big city all by himself?"

"He'll be with Sabriel," Baba said.

"Your bachelor brother, who's never so much as held a baby, let alone cared for a child full-time?"

"He's a doctor," Baba said. "And he held Ziva and Pesah plenty of times when they were—"

"I don't like the idea of him being so far away," Ziva's mother said.

Ziva's lower lip hardened. What did her mother care if Pesah was in Samkarsh? Pesah was right there in the garden, and Ziva had never seen her mother visit him. At least if he were in Samkarsh, on the other side of the empire by the Black Sea, their mother would have a viable excuse for not visiting him.

"We don't need to decide now," Baba said. "We have a month to think about it. And to ask Pesah what he wants to do."

Ziva's mother scoffed. "Well, we can't ask Ziva."

Ziva bristled.

"She'll pitch an absolute fit," her mother continued.

Baba paused for a long time. "Ziva is a good girl. She'll do what's best for Pesah."

In the dim wardrobe, Ziva frowned. She'd do anything for Pesah if it was good for him . . . but was sending him to Samkarsh actually the best for him? The journey there was long. The city itself was big and rowdy, Uncle Sabriel often said, and then he'd tell them a story about how a sailor had walked into his office with a fishhook in his face, or he'd pulled out five of someone's teeth, or someone had been kicked by a horse and the bruises over their broken ribs were perfectly in the shape of the horse's hooves. Pesah was enthralled by these stories. Ziva was normally queasy by the end.

In a pouty voice, Ziva's mother said, "She got mad at me this morning when I told her about the party."

Baba sighed. "You know she doesn't like crowds, Leah."

"It's not a crowd!" Ziva's mother said. "It's a birthday party!"

Baba sighed. Ziva knew he understood, even if her mother didn't. Parties were just organized crowds, and crowds were the worst.

"Still," Baba said, and from the tone, Ziva could tell he was smiling.

Ziva's mother huffed. "You two. Cut from the same cloth."

"We can't help liking the quiet moments," Baba said. "I'll let you get back to party planning. Where's Ziva?"

"Oh, who knows?" Ziva's mother said, exasperated. "In your office, rooting around in your ledgers. Or with Pesah, doing exactly what we told her not to."

Ziva's face felt hot. They knew about her going to see Pesah? They hadn't said anything to her about it. Maybe that meant they'd finally realized she was the person doing all the real work for him.

"She hasn't been in my office for a long time," Baba said.

Ziva's mother continued like he hadn't said anything. "When she scolded me for the party, she ran off and said she was going to the market. The market! All on her own!"

"She knows the market."

"It's uncivilized," Ziva's mother said. "At least she has the sense not to go out alone in the dark, with the sheydim and the mazzikim."

Ziva could imagine Baba's face, very carefully keeping his eyes from rolling. He didn't believe in demons and imps the way her mother did. Ziva didn't want to believe in them, but when the sun set and shadows deepened, it was hard not to remember her mother's and grandmother's stories about demons in the night that would set upon an unsuspecting traveler.

Baba said, "Ziva wouldn't go out alone at night, Leah."

"Maybe she needs a handmaid to reel her in."

Another long, long pause from Baba. "We'll see. I'll go find her. Enjoy the party planning."

The sound of a chaste kiss planted on someone's cheek or forehead, and then Baba's heavy footsteps out of the room. Ziva's mother huffed a couple times, paced, and then she left as well.

Ziva waited a few breaths and then crawled out of the wardrobe. Her face was hot and probably as red as the ribbon at the end of her braid. She'd been gripping the ceramic bowl in her hand so tightly, she had a line across her palm from its rim. With a frown, she set the ceramic bowl on the vanity's top. She grabbed two metal bowls full of jewelry—rings, bracelets, and baubles to hang off brow bands—and tipped them out onto the vanity's surface. The pieces of jewelry spilled around the ceramic bowl, making *tak-tak-tak* sounds as they rolled around on the wood. She gave each bowl a shake to make sure she'd emptied out every last piece of stupid shiny jewelry, and then she exited the room, metal bowls in hand.

SEVEN

PESAH WAS SITTING UP IN BED coughing when Ziva got back. His eyes were watering, and the wet cough rattled Ziva's own chest. She set her items from the market, along with the wine and the bowls, down at the laboratory. Then she went to his bed to pat him on the back, as if solid enough pats would knock loose whatever was settled in his lungs that made him cough.

When he finally stopped, he said, "Thanks, Ziva." He cleared his throat. "I had an idea while you were gone."

Ziva brightened. "An idea about a cure?"

He shook his head. "No. I thought, you know, what if instead of doing things for me all day, we do something for you?"

She scoffed. "Like what?"

"I don't know," Pesah said. "Maybe Baba will let us read some of his old ledgers. Or finding some kourabiedes at the market. Or, um, just going to find a quiet spot on the river to throw stones." He shrugged in the direction of the pebble-heavy bookshelves.

"I don't care about that stuff anymore," Ziva said, only half lying.

"You care about *all* of that stuff," Pesah said.

Ziva huffed. "Yeah, I guess. But I care about you a lot more. I can read books and eat cookies when you're better. And we can *both* skip stones."

He stared at the rocks on the bookshelf for a long time. "Ziva—"

"No one knew what crop-leek or spear-leek was," she said, tired of the conversation distracting her from curing him before Uncle Sabriel arrived. "So I got regular leek, and some onions."

Pesah sighed, then nodded. Slowly, he said, "We'll see if it can work anyway."

"Yeah," Ziva said, her eyes falling upon the bandage-wrapped finger she'd amputated that morning. "How does your hand feel?"

Pesah looked down at it. "Fine, I guess. I can't feel anything, if that's what you're asking."

"It was," she said. She almost wished he *could* feel something. If he could feel something, that would mean the disease was going away. It would mean he was getting better.

She helped him into his chair and pushed it across the little house to the laboratory. There, she set Pesah's favorite books around him, and opened the Byzantine pamphlet for him to the recipe page. Then Ziva went to the laboratory bench, and while she sharpened a knife, she said, "I brought two bowls, because I couldn't tell which one was brass."

Pesah leaned forward so he could examine the bowls. "They're both brass."

"What?" Ziva asked, pausing in sharpening her knife. "But they're different colors."

"One's tarnished a little," Pesah said. "It oxidized."

"Should we use the one that isn't oxidized?" Ziva asked, not entirely sure what "oxidized" even meant.

Pesah shrugged. "I don't know if it matters. But we might as well use the one that isn't."

Ziva nodded and picked up the bowl that Pesah indicated. Then, in their usual method, they began to create the medicine. Pesah narrated, drawing knowledge from the recipe, the books, his brilliant brain. Ziva acted as his hands: chopping, crushing, grinding, mixing. When he'd reach over to try to touch something, she'd swat him away.

When they were done, Pesah's house was thick with the pungent odor of the medicine. Ziva gave the medicine—onion, leek, bull's gall, and wine—a good final stir, and then turned to her brother.

"What now?"

"Now it sits for nine days," Pesah said.

"Covered, I hope," Ziva said, wrinkling her nose.

Pesah checked the recipe. "It doesn't say."

"We should cover it," Ziva said. "So you don't wind up smelling like you're turning into an onion."

"Eh," Pesah said. He leaned forward to study the medicine more closely. "It looks very unimpressive so far. We'll see what we have in nine days."

"And while we wait," Ziva said, thinking of Uncle Sabriel's letter, "we'll keep looking for other medicine. Right?"

Pesah said, "Or we could do something else." He coughed: wet and hoarse, but not the prolonged fit that was becoming more and more common. He reached for one of his books, which Ziva handed to him, and he read it aloud, mentioning things of importance for Ziva to take note of in his ledger.

They did this for hours, and only stopped when someone knocked on the door.

"Who is it?" Pesah called while Ziva ducked out of sight of the front door and window.

"It's Setareh," came the voice from outside.

Pesah lifted his eyebrows at Ziva. Normally, Ziva would have hidden better, but hearing what her parents had said about her earlier that morning changed things. They knew she was here. She didn't have to sneak anymore. She glanced at the brass bowl filled with the smelliest medicine Ziva had ever been involved with, and then at Pesah.

"I'll answer it," Ziva said.

Pesah's eyes widened. "What?"

Ziva set his ledger down and jumped up, opening the door to let late afternoon sunlight stream in. Setareh stood by herself out there, hands clasped in front of her belly, and looking not at all surprised to see Ziva.

"Your mother's been looking for you," Setareh said.

Ziva crossed her arms. "She couldn't come here herself?"

Setareh ignored Ziva's snark and looked past her to Pesah. She smiled and said, "*Tavalodet mobarak*, Pesah-*joon*."

Pesah stayed where he was by the laboratory. "Thank you, Setareh," he said.

Setareh returned her attention to Ziva. "It's almost time for your party. Come get dressed."

Ziva planted her feet squarely on the stone floor. "We're working on something."

"You can finish it later," Setareh said kindly. "You have guests arriving soon. You don't want to offend them."

On the one hand, Ziva didn't care if she offended her guests. Who would they be, anyway? Other girls her age who didn't ever play with her, and annoying boys like Reuven who were supposed to be candidates for her destiny? She wasn't interested in either.

But.

Baba would probably invite the other judges.

Ziva could talk to them. Impress them. Make them see that she had what it took to be a judge herself, like Devorah the Prophetess. Devorah had been a woman, and she had been a great judge and defeated a whole army. Ziva touched her brooch softly. Maybe one of them would sponsor her education or take her on as an apprentice.

After Pesah was cured, of course.

She said, "I'll get ready."

Setareh looked relieved that Ziva hadn't argued. "Wonderful."

"As soon as I get Pesah dressed," Ziva said.

Now Setareh's mouth tightened. "Ziva—"

"It's his birthday too, Setareh."

"*Ziva,*" Setareh repeated. "Do you think that's wise?"

"It's *fair,*" Ziva said, bristling under her kaftan at the way everyone treated Pesah, shoving him aside like he was already gone. "It's his birthday too, and he deserves to be at a party."

"Please be reasonable," Setareh said, closing her eyes. "Your mother—"

"Will be so happy to see Pesah," Ziva said, putting her fists on her hips. "Since she never comes to see him here."

Setareh's nostrils flared but she said nothing else. She shook her head and walked away, and Pesah said, "I don't have to go to the party, Ziva."

"It's your birthday, too." Ziva shut the door and started to tidy up Pesah's house, while he remained in his chair and clutched the book against his lap.

Pesah said softly, "No one will speak to me. They never do."

"I'll stay by you," she said. "If they want to say something to me, they'll have to say it to you, too."

He was quiet for a few moments. "They're all going to stare at me."

"If they do that, I'll make a fool of myself somewhere else, so they have something more interesting to look at."

Pesah laughed, coughed, and said, "I wonder if, before we were born, you pulled all the fire out of me for yourself."

Ziva stopped her tidying and looked back at Pesah. "Fire?"

"Yes, fire," Pesah said. "Passion and spunk and stubbornness. You've got so much of it, and I've got none."

"Maybe what happened was that you took all the brilliance," Ziva said. "And I had to fill the space up with something."

Pesah laughed softly. "You're brilliant too, Ziva."

She smiled, tight-lipped, knowing he was just being nice by saying that. It was okay, though, that she wasn't as smart as he was. "I'm going to go get dressed, and I'll be back to get you," Ziva said. "Okay?"

"Okay," Pesah said. He went back to reading his book, and Ziva hurried to her room to get dressed.

EIGHT

ZIVA'S MOTHER HAD LAID OUT something special for Ziva to wear. As Ziva picked up the Byzantine dress with its loud colors and odorous tassels, Ziva scrunched up her face. She wanted to just wear a nice kaftan, not this orange-and-blue abomination. There were even matching blue slippers on the floor instead of boots.

No.

Ziva would *not* wear this.

She tossed the dress back on her bed as she marched to her wardrobe. She flung the doors open, and was met with a note drawn on parchment that was pinned to one of the kaftans. It was in Setareh's graceful handwriting: *Don't you dare!*

Ziva scoffed out loud and said, "How did she know?"

Then she turned to look at the Byzantine dress. After squinting at it for several breaths, she shut her wardrobe and trudged to the bed. As she changed from her kaftan into the dress, she rationalized that she was already doing something that would make her mother angry—bringing Pesah to the party—and maybe by wearing this dress, her mother wouldn't screech so loud.

As she pulled the dress on, she noticed a small, pale patch of skin by her wrist. She poked it. No pain. Nothing. She must have spilled something on it in Pesah's laboratory.

The dress was on. It was horrible.

The slippers were on. They were horrible, too.

She pinned the date palm brooch to the top of the dress. That made it a little better. But it was still terrible.

Ziva threw a longing glance at her boots by her wardrobe as she exited her room and returned to Pesah's house. The dress was long, all the way down to her toes, and she felt like she was going to trip over it. It dragged on the ground. Did Byzantine ladies not care that their dresses dragged and got all ragged and dirty? Maybe in Byzantium, they kept the ground cleaner than they did in Atil. Ziva didn't know much about Byzantium, except that it was to the south on the other side of the Black Sea, and it was the Christian sometimes-enemy of Khazaria, and that the biggest building in the whole world was there.

As she did her best not to trip over the dress, she heard a deep, rumbling voice say her name. Only one person in their household had a voice like that.

Baba approached Ziva as she waited for him in the hallway. He smiled at her from under his big beard and said,

"Happy birthday, Ziva." He extended a hand with a small gift in it, without any of the pomp and fanfare that her mother would have included. She knew even before she opened it that it was a book.

"I've kept a journal every day of my life since I became a bar mitzvah," Baba said. "And I thought you'd like your very own journal to start."

A blank journal was infinitely better than an ugly Byzantine dress. She hugged him around his midsection and said, "Thank you, Baba."

He kissed her on top of her head. "Where are you headed, looking so pretty?"

"To Pesah's house," Ziva said, noting but ignoring Baba's peaked brows at her comment. "And I'm not pretty. I look like a fool."

"You look like a lady," Baba said. "What are you going to see Pesah for?"

"Birthday things," Ziva said.

Baba nodded, face troubled. Probably worried about breaking the news to her that Pesah was going to live with Uncle Sabriel in Samkarsh soon. But Baba didn't know about their cure, and he didn't know Pesah was about to be healthy again. He wouldn't have to live with Uncle Sabriel after all.

Ziva didn't mention any of that. It would be a New Year surprise. So instead she asked, "Are you on your way to see him, too? We can walk together."

Baba blinked, then said, "Yes, I was. How did you know?"

Ziva shrugged and said nothing.

Baba offered his elbow to her. "Let's go see Pesah."

She took his elbow and went. They didn't speak. They didn't have to. Ziva and Baba liked the quiet between conversations.

Ziva and Baba arrived at Pesah's house. He was by his window again, reading, and when he glanced up and saw them, he sounded surprised when he said, "Hello, Baba."

"Happy birthday, Pesah." Baba pulled another journal out of his kaftan and handed it to Pesah, who took it carefully in gauze-wrapped fingers. He repeated what he'd said to Ziva, and added, "And even though you've got a year until you'll be a bar mitzvah, I think you're mature enough to keep a journal, hm?"

Pesah said, "I think so, Baba."

Baba motioned to the open book in Pesah's lap. "Greek?"

Pesah nodded. "It's my gift from Mama. She thought I'd like another Greek cooking book."

Baba nodded with approval, but Ziva stuck her tongue out. A cooking book for Pesah's birthday gift? Maybe a Greek mathematics or science book. But cooking? Pesah couldn't cook, and he wouldn't even if he could. Plus, he already had a Greek cooking book. So their mother had gotten him a second book in a topic he didn't even care about. Ziva's mother just wasn't at all knowledgeable about her children.

"Plus, she brought some baklava," Pesah said, motioning to a platter with the sweet, flaky pastries on it.

Ziva eyed the baklava. Probably extras from the party.

Baba said, "Maybe we can have a special treat after dinner tonight, Pesah. You and me. I'll bring you some cookies."

Pesah's bandages shifted up as he smiled, but Ziva found herself frowning. Cookies and conversation, she was sure, and she thought she knew the topic: going to Samkarsh with Uncle Sabriel.

"I'd love that, Baba," Pesah said.

"Good," Baba said. "Good. Now Ziva, let's get going to your party, hm?"

Ziva balked, but managed to coolly say, "I'll be there soon, Baba. I have to give Pesah his birthday gift."

Baba looked like he was about to say something, but he walked away instead. As soon as he was gone, Pesah looked at Ziva and burst into laughter.

"What?" Ziva demanded.

Pesah managed to say, "The . . . dress!"

"Oh, be quiet," Ziva grumbled as she walked into Pesah's house.

"What *is* that?" Pesah asked through laughter.

Ziva huffed. "It's Mother's attempt to turn me into a smaller version of herself." She scowled as Pesah continued to giggle under his wrappings.

He managed to get ahold of himself, stifling his laughs, and he said, "Ziva, you look very pretty. Even in those colors."

Ziva checked Pesah's bandages over, making sure all of his lesions and scars were covered. "Do I look serious, though? Like I'd make a good apprentice to the other judges?"

"Of course you'd make a good apprentice."

"Do I look like that, though?" Ziva asked. "Or do I look like a fool?"

Pesah patted her hand. "You look like you're capable of withstanding humiliation with grace and poise in the name of social decorum."

Ziva sighed. "Let's get this party over with."

Pesah nodded, and she caught a flash of apprehension in his eye and stepped behind the chair. She leaned against the chair with her hips and squeezed his shoulder, then pushed him out of his house and into the afternoon garden. She could hear people arriving on the other side of the house at the main door, and sighed. Pesah shifted in his chair.

"I don't know about this, Ziva," he said.

"It's your birthday, too," she said. "You deserve to be at this party." She thought of her mother's face when Ziva said she hated parties, and when she accused her mother of keeping Pesah locked away because he was ugly. Crocodile tears had sparkled in her eyes. More upset that someone was chastising her, rather than upset that she kept her son locked away like some kind of dirty secret. Then Ziva's mind jumped to the conversation between her mother and Baba. Sending Pesah to Samkarsh to live with Uncle Sabriel. Her mother had been right about one thing, anyway: that

Ziva would pitch a fit. She intended to if they tried to send Pesah away. Not because she didn't think Uncle Sabriel could take care of Pesah, but because even the thought of being apart from her brother made Ziva's heart ache and made the breath stop in her lungs. They had never been apart. Ever. And she wasn't going to start now.

Pesah hesitated, then said, "I do miss seeing people."

Even the thought of being at a party exhausted Ziva, but for Pesah's benefit, she smiled and tried to sound cheerful when she said, "Well, let's go see the people, then."

NINE

ZIVA FOLLOWED THE SOUND of voices and laughter to the open air hall that Ziva's mother had decorated for the party. Tall vases full of flowers sat on long tables festooned with platters of food interspersed with carafes of various drinks. The reflecting pool at the center of the room twinkled with the reflections of hundreds of candles and lanterns hung around the room.

As soon as Ziva wheeled Pesah into the hall, Setareh was upon them. Very sternly, she said just one word: "Ziva."

Ziva dug her heels into the floor and lifted her chin up. "It's his birthday, too."

Pesah slunk down in the wheelchair. "I can go, Setareh."

Setareh looked down at Pesah and her stern, exasperated face softened. "No, Pesah-*joon*." She sighed. "You stay. But let me prepare your mother."

Ziva let go of the wheelchair to motion to her dress, and said, "She already got her way. If she doesn't want Pesah here, then she doesn't want me here, either."

Setareh didn't respond to Ziva. She just walked away, shaking her head, and Ziva grasped the wheelchair's handles again in sweating fingers.

Pesah, still slouched in the chair, said, "Mama's going to be angry."

"Let her be," Ziva said, and she pushed Pesah to the long table with food. "What do you want to eat?"

Pesah pointed out the foods he wanted as guests entered the hall. Ziva heard some angry sounds from her mother across the hall, and her face grew hot in anticipation of a scolding. But she never came over, so Ziva dished up Pesah's food uninterrupted. She didn't get any for herself. Not yet. She didn't want to have her mouth full when one of Baba's judge friends came to wish her a happy birthday. She wanted a free mouth with which to talk.

Pesah lowered the plate to his lap and gripped its edges with bandaged fingers as Ziva pushed him to sit by the reflecting pool. Baba stood next to Ziva's mother by the main door, and Ziva looked up in time to catch Baba watching her with a frown behind his long beard. She held his stare until he looked away.

"I don't think Baba's happy to see me here," Pesah said. He was looking at Baba too, eyes worried.

"He is," Ziva said. "I bet he's just frowning because he has to hear all her complaining." She nodded her chin toward their mother.

"Maybe I should let Setareh take me back to my room," Pesah said.

"No way." Ziva's hand tightened on the wheelchair handle. She wasn't going to let them chase Pesah away.

One of the other judges walked in, bowed to Ziva's mother and father, and then turned to the boy who walked in beside him.

Another judge came in, also with a boy Ziva's age in tow.

Ziva narrowed her eyes at the two boys. The sons of the judges. Surely, they had been invited because this was a birthday party, and inviting other children to play games with made sense.

Then the rabbi came in, with Reuven beside him. No Shmuel.

Ziva realized there were no girls her age at the party yet.

Well . . . it was still early.

But she didn't think there would be any girls her age at this party.

Neither did she think there would be any boys younger than thirteen.

Her mother was trying to force a destiny meeting.

Ziva frowned to herself until Pesah said, "The dolma is good."

She glanced at him. He was still slumped, like if he pressed himself hard enough into his chair, he could disappear into it. He held the dolma awkwardly in bandaged fingers, keeping his eyes downcast.

Despite being in the center of the room where everyone could see her, Ziva was not approached by anyone. Not for birthday wishes. Not by any of the boys to flirt awkwardly. Not by any of their fathers to evaluate her for a future match. And not by her mother, who seethed by the entrance, or her father, who had a hand set on her mother's shoulder.

Then Reuven ben Kohen peeled off from a small group of boys who were speaking and casting furtive glances at Ziva and Pesah, and strode toward her. As he neared, Pesah said softly, "I don't feel good. I want to go back to my room."

"Okay," Ziva said. Perfect timing. She grasped the chair's handles as Reuven said, "Ziva! Pesah! Happy birthday!"

Pesah peered up at Reuven, squinting against a headache, and Ziva said as coldly as she could, "We're leaving."

Reuven stood in front of Pesah's chair, barring Ziva's escape. "Ziva, don't go. I, um, want to apologize for—"

"Pesah isn't feeling well," Ziva said, completely not interested in the apology that had likely been demanded by Reuven's father, turning the chair to go around Reuven.

He stepped in front again. "I'm trying to say I'm sorry for what happened at the market."

"I know," Ziva said, saying every word slowly so he'd understand. "And I'm trying to take Pesah back to his room because he isn't feeling well."

"So, your medicine didn't work, then?"

Ziva ground her teeth together. Of course he'd assume she messed it up. Of course he'd rub that in her face. What would he say next? That this was proof she should give up on being a judge, too? "Move, Reuven."

Pesah looked up at Ziva, face still pinched with pain. "How does he know about the medicine?"

Before Ziva could explain, Reuven said, "My father told me your parents are sending him away. To a colony in Samkarsh."

Ziva stared at him, pulse pounding in her ears. A colony? The letter had said Pesah would live with Uncle Sabriel, not go to a colony. Right? They'd never send Pesah to a colony: a walled city or an island where he was sent to die alone with others who were sick. Never.

Ziva's hands tightened on the chair's handles. "They would never."

Pesah's breath hitched, like he was crying. But when Ziva leaned down to look at him, he was just squinting against a headache, as if someone was shining a bright light in his eyes.

"Move, Reuven." Ziva tried to use her father's stern, commanding tone. "Can't you see he's in pain?"

Reuven didn't look at Pesah. "Have a servant take him. You should stay here."

She didn't like his attitude. Not one bit. Where did he get off, telling her what she needed to do? But before she could shove him out of the way, Pesah sat up straight, threw his head back, and gasped in a hard breath.

"Pesah?" Ziva put her hands on his shoulders. He was tensed up beneath her, like every muscle was clenching at once.

Reuven cringed away, and the disgust and alarm on his face were almost too much for Ziva to tolerate. But then he gasped out, "What's *wrong* with him?" and *that was it*.

Ziva's fist connected with Reuven's nose before she even realized she was swinging. He yelped, staggered back, and tripped over the edge of the reflecting pool. Into the water he went, splashing it up and over the sides. Floating candles bobbed and capsized, spilling onto the floor with the water.

Pesah was stock-still, hands splayed, the careful gauze applied to them unraveling. His eyes shone like they had shards of starlight in them, and his mouth gaped under the bandages on his face. Tears streamed, soaking the gauze on his face, as his eyes ticked around and around, like he was taking in a flock of birds flying all around him. But there was nothing in the air that he could possibly be looking at.

He whispered something, his words barely reaching Ziva's ears over the commotion going on around her. She could hear Reuven howling and her mother yelling and the deep voices of judges and the rabbi, but she ignored them all. So she could hear Pesah whisper, "*Malach ha-mavet.*"

"Pesah," Ziva whispered, voice catching in her mouth. She had no idea what Pesah was saying.

Then Setareh was there, grabbing Pesah's chair handles and pushing him toward the exit.

Ziva tried to follow, but a hand gripping her arm stopped her. She turned, ready to swing again, but it was her father holding her. His face was red and furious. When he spoke, his words came out like hot coals.

"My office," he spat. "Now."

TEN

BABA'S OFFICE WAS NORMALLY a safe place for Ziva. She would sneak into it and go through his ledgers and law books and even furtively run her hands over the dark robes he wore to court, imagining herself in those very robes one day, sitting with other judges.

But today, as Baba crowded her into the office and slammed the door shut behind them, that safety scattered to the winds.

He opened his mouth to start speaking several times, but shut it, swallowing his words. He couldn't figure out what to say to her. Ziva stood still, fists at her sides, shoulders back, chin out, ready for the dressing-down she was surely in for.

Then Baba spoke. Quiet rage. "Describe to me your thought process, Ziva, that would make you get into a fight with Reuven ben Kohen."

"He made fun of Pesah!" Ziva yelled, then calmed herself. She could be quiet, too. "What was I supposed to do? Just let him say terrible things?"

"You're supposed to walk away, Ziva," Baba said. "Not hit the rabbi's son in the nose so hard he falls into the pool and bleeds everywhere."

"Maybe he should learn how to dodge a punch!" Ziva said, satisfied that she'd made Reuven's nose bleed.

Baba seemed to expand. His fury was like a peacock's tail, rising up behind him. "This is out of control."

Ziva still faced him with her chin out, but her arms trembled.

"I shouldn't have let this go for so long," Baba said. "Sabriel told me. I should have listened sooner."

Ziva's trembling intensified. "Uncle Sabriel told you what?"

Baba stared at her long and stern. He was using his full judge-face: serious and . . . well, judging. The blue of his eyes seemed to darken to black. "I'm sending Pesah away."

Ziva couldn't speak for a moment. She had overheard him tell her mother that Pesah would go to Uncle Sabriel's. Reuven had said a colony. "Where?"

"Samkarsh," Baba said.

Ziva swallowed hard. "To live with Uncle Sabriel?"

"To live in one of the colonies," he said, and Ziva felt like all the air had been slammed out of her lungs.

"To *what?*" Ziva yelled, her words shooting out like vomit.

"To live without being stared at," Baba continued. "Without people like Reuven to ridicule him."

"To die!" Ziva screamed.

"He's going to die anyway!" Baba's voice cracked as it boomed, echoing around the room. It knocked the fight out of Ziva, and her trembling ceased as her arms went limp. Baba swallowed several times. His eyes glistened. He pressed his palms against his chest and loosely gripped the folds of his kaftan with his fingers. He let his hands drop to his sides, listless. "He's going to die, Ziva. There's nothing we can do."

"Uncle Sabriel said . . ." Ziva hurriedly wiped a tear from her cheek. "He said people like Pesah can live for a long time."

"He also said Pesah is one of the worst cases he's ever seen," Baba said. "And he said Pesah needs to live away from us. That's why he lives in his own house. He could make us sick."

"Pesah wouldn't do that," Ziva argued, thinking, this wasn't the time to point out that she was clearly immune, since she'd been sleeping in his house ever since it had been built.

"He wouldn't mean to," Baba said. "Sabriel doesn't know how the disease spreads, but they think through touch perhaps. They don't know. But it does spread. He's afraid for us. For you."

Tears kept coming. No matter how fast Ziva wiped them away, they came back, wetting her face. "You can't send him away. He'll die all by himself."

"There are other people at the colonies."

"But they're not his family," Ziva said. Her head was throbbing. There was so much pressure. Like there were so many tears they couldn't all get out fast enough, so they were backing up, filling her head. "He can't die without his family."

"If he makes us sick?" Baba asked. "If he makes *you* sick? And then in a few years, you die, too?"

Ziva shook her head. Pesah wouldn't make her sick. He wouldn't. And even if he did, they were going to find a cure. The medicine in his house would work. Pesah was the smartest person in Atil. Maybe all of Khazaria. Byzantium, too. If anyone could find a cure, Pesah could.

Baba said, "How do you think Pesah would feel if you got sick?"

Ziva crossed her arms and hunched her shoulders in. He would feel terrible. But that wasn't going to happen. It wasn't.

Baba set a hand on Ziva's shoulder. "I don't think you should see him anymore."

She looked up at him, tears still streaming. "What?"

"I know you go visit him, Ziva," Baba said. "And I . . . I didn't have the heart to tell you to stop. But now—"

"Who's going to take care of him?" Ziva blurted out.

Baba said, "The servants do that."

"No, they don't!" Ziva backed up to the door. "He needs someone to bandage him up, and they don't know how to do it. He'll get an infection, Baba. He'll—"

He'll die.

He's going to die anyway.

She shook her head again, banishing the voices, and then wrenched the office door open. Baba yelled her name but she ignored him, running full speed down the hallway, headed straight to Pesah's house.

ELEVEN

PESAH'S HOUSE WAS DARK. He was in bed. Part of Ziva wanted to leave him to rest, but a stronger part of her needed to talk to him. So she crept in, leaving the lights out, and sat on the foot of his bed.

He stirred, peering at her. "Ziva?"

"Yes," she said. "Pesah, I'm so sorry."

He sat up, coughing as he did. It was still wet and deep in his chest. Once he stopped, he said, "It's okay, Ziva."

"No it isn't," she said. "It was stupid. You didn't want to be there, even. I shouldn't have taken you." She frowned, remembering Reuven's face, gnarled with disgust that Pesah was seizing. *What's wrong with him?* He'd spat the words out like they were poison, like they tasted foul. Like Pesah wasn't a human being anymore.

He could make us sick. Baba's words, from Uncle Sabriel.

Ziva wiped new tears from her cheeks and said, "Baba is going to send you away."

Pesah was quiet, his raspy breathing turning into a wet cough before he said, "Where?"

"Samkarsh," Ziva mumbled. "To a colony."

The twins were silent, sitting a foot apart but adrift in different worlds. Ziva didn't know what Pesah was thinking, exactly, but she'd spent every day with him for their whole lives, so she had an idea. She knew he was weighing the good versus bad. He was analyzing the situation. He was thinking about the greater good, and how he could improve the situation, and—

Ziva was just trying to keep herself from screaming.

Pesah nodded. "That's probably best."

"No it isn't," Ziva said. "It's the worst."

"Did Baba say when?" Pesah asked.

Ziva snorted, remembering the discussion Baba had had with Ziva's mother in their bedroom. "Uncle Sabriel is coming here for the New Year. He's going to take you back with him afterward. So . . . a month?"

Pesah's eyes shone again with the same eerie light from the hall earlier. "Rosh Hashanah?"

"After that," Ziva said. "You'll still be with us on Rosh Hashanah."

Pesah was silent, looking down at his hands, fingers tugging on the end of his gauze wrappings. When he spoke, he did so without looking up.

"I have to tell you something."

Ziva nodded. She needed to tell him something, too. That Baba wouldn't let her tend to him anymore. That he was not only going to go to Samkarsh to live in a colony with other lepers until he died from an infection or from the cough that rattled his chest, but that he wouldn't be allowed to see Ziva while he was still in Atil. But she'd let him speak first. "Tell me."

Pesah glanced at the door, then at Ziva. "I . . . it sounds so ridiculous. I thought it was just a fever coming or something. But Rosh Hashanah . . . It can't be a coincidence."

"What can't?" Ziva said.

"I saw something."

"Something?" Ziva asked. "Like what something?"

Pesah was quiet for a long time, staring at his bandaged hands. "I don't really know."

Ziva scooted closer to him. "Well . . . just tell me what it looked like."

"That's the thing," Pesah said. "It wasn't something. It was—" He groaned, irritated, and hit his hands against the bed. "Rosh Hashanah."

"Rosh Hashanah?"

"Yes," Pesah said. "I was standing on a road. A blue road through a red land. But I wasn't really. It wasn't a road."

Ziva stared. "When were you standing on a road?"

"I wasn't," Pesah said. "I *saw myself* standing on a road."

"A blue road?" Ziva asked.

Pesah nodded. "One moment, Reuven was standing in front of me talking about our medicine, and the next moment, my head split apart." He put his palms on either side of his head. "And I wasn't there anymore. It was all dark, and then I was standing on the blue road on Rosh Hashanah. And there was . . . someone. Someone was on the road with me."

Ziva's heart thumped in her chest like someone beating a drum too hard. "Pesah, did you see a vision?"

He shook his head. "I hope not."

"Who was with you?" Ziva asked.

"I don't know," Pesah said, voice like a whisper. "Eyes. Too many eyes."

"You said something," Ziva said, leaning closer. "You said *malach ha-mavet*. What does that mean?"

Pesah looked up at her, face paling under his bandages. "I said that?"

Ziva nodded. "What is it?"

Pesah looked around his room, like he was checking to make sure no one else was there, and he said, "*Malach ha-mavet* is Hebrew. It means 'Angel of Death.'"

A chill passed between them, like someone had left a window open on a winter day.

"You said it," Ziva whispered.

"I don't remember saying anything," Pesah mumbled at his lap.

Ziva stared into the deepening darkness in the corners of the room. "What did the Angel of Death do? Just stand on the road?"

"I walked to him," Pesah said. "He had something I needed." He wouldn't look up from his lap. "I didn't know it was the Angel of Death. It just looked like a man with too many eyes."

"What did he have?" Ziva asked.

"I don't know," Pesah said. "When I got to him and I touched him, he—" Pesah coughed, wet and wracking, and Ziva scooted toward him so she could pat his back. She thought of what Baba had said, what Uncle Sabriel feared. That Pesah would infect her. She patted him anyway.

When Pesah stopped coughing, he said, "He grabbed my wrist, and then I woke up in bed."

"Setareh brought you," Ziva said. Her mind whirred as she continued to pat Pesah's back. A blue road in a red land. Rosh Hashanah. The Angel of Death, a man with too many eyes.

She didn't know what Pesah thought about this vision, but Ziva had one word running around in her head: *prophecy.*

Ziva was not an authority on prophecies. She wasn't sure this even counted as a prophecy, because prophecies were from Hashem. Plus, they were supposed to be important information to be shared with everyone, not just something about one person.

Maybe not a prophecy, then. A vision of the future. A premonition of his own death. Because that's what it was, for sure. Ziva didn't think Pesah's vision happening on Rosh Hashanah was a coincidence. Uncle Sabriel would be taking Pesah to Samkarsh around Rosh Hashanah, and Ziva was barred from caring for Pesah. Either Pesah was going to die in their home from neglect, or he was going to die on the way to Samkarsh with Uncle Sabriel.

No.

She wouldn't let that happen.

Ziva looked toward the medicine they had concocted earlier. Beside it sat the pamphlet from Byzantium where Pesah had found the recipe.

Byzantium. A great nation. Constantinople, a city of wonders. And doctors. Constantinople had hundreds of doctors, Ziva bet. One of them had to know a cure for Pesah.

"I have an idea," Ziva said as the door opened and the yellow light of a lantern lit the room.

Baba's voice said, "Ziva. It's time to say goodbye."

TWELVE

ZIVA STOOD BY PESAH'S BED, fists at her sides. "Good-bye," she said pointedly to Baba and whomever was with him.

Baba sighed deeply, softly. "Say goodbye to Pesah."

Pesah sat on his bed, looking like he wished he could vanish, and his big blue eyes were confused. "Goodbye?"

"There's no reason to say goodbye," Ziva said.

Baba's jaw clenched, he took a breath, and he addressed Pesah. "Sabriel says you could make Ziva sick, Pesah."

Pesah blinked slowly a few times. "Sick?"

"She could catch what you have," Baba said.

"Baba, stop!" Ziva said. "Pesah isn't going to make me sick. Right, Pesah?"

Baba continued. "I don't think she should come see you anymore."

"I have to!" Ziva shouted. "Who else is going to? You?" She pointed at Baba. "Or you?" Her finger found her mother now, peering around Baba. "You *never* come see him!"

Before she could continue, Pesah put a soft hand on her arm, quieting her. "If Uncle Sabriel is right, then maybe you shouldn't come."

Ziva shook her head. "But what if he's wrong?" she said, knowing Pesah would never accept that Uncle Sabriel could be wrong. She wanted to ask about his vision, about *malach ha-mavet*, but not while their parents were standing right there. Baba was staring pointedly at Pesah and their mother still hadn't even come fully into the room, and Pesah pulled his bandaged hand away from Ziva like he *was* going to make her sick, and it all made her want to scream.

Then, suddenly, her mother did enter the room. But she wasn't looking at Pesah or even Ziva. She was looking at the makeshift laboratory, where the result of their day's labor rested in the brass bowls.

"My jewelry bowls!" she said, pointing. Her face turned red. She crossed to the laboratory, and Ziva ran to intercept her.

"Don't touch those!" Ziva ordered.

But her mother never listened to her, and she wasn't about to start now. She grabbed the bowl closest to her and tore off the cover, grimacing. "What have you *done* to it?"

"We needed it for Pesah's medicine!" Ziva said, reaching to snatch it back.

But her mother wasn't giving it up. "Is this just pounded-up onions?"

"It's *medicine*," Ziva said.

Her mother grabbed the second bowl and said, "This is ridiculous. Out of control. These are *my bowls*, Ziva! For my jewelry!"

"Who cares about your stupid jewelry?" Ziva yelled, and she tried to grab the bowls from her mother.

"Ziva!" Baba hollered from the door.

Too late.

The medicine sloshed inside, and then one bowl slipped from her mother's hand. It hit the floor with a *clang* and a splatter, sending the concoction of wine, onion, and bull's gall all over the front of Ziva's and her mother's dresses. Her mother looked down at the mess and let out a high-pitched exhalation, and Ziva took the chance to grab the other bowl away from her.

But Baba was there. While Ziva's mother cried over the loss of an ugly dress, her father grabbed the bowl out of Ziva's hand, strode to the door, and before Ziva could beg him not to, dumped the medicine out on the ground.

"Baba!" Ziva screamed. "That was medicine! It could have helped—"

"Enough, Ziva!" Baba boomed, and the room went silent. Even Ziva's mother no longer wailed about her ruined dress. "It isn't going to help. *Nothing* is going to help. I've indulged you for too long. Go to your room. *Go*," he said more forcefully when she opened her mouth to argue.

Pesah was still on his bed, blankets pulled up to his chin, watching with wide, wet eyes. He met Ziva's eyes with his for a moment, and gave her a tiny nod.

Go.

So she did. She ran, and didn't stop until she got to her room. Her head felt so hot she was afraid her hair would start smoking at any moment. She tore the stupid Byzantine dress off, threw the useless slippers against the wall, and threw herself on her bed. That lasted for about thirty seconds, and then Ziva was up again, pacing, pulling on her nightgown, pacing more.

Byzantium.

Baba had a lot of horses. Ziva wasn't an expert like her ancestors had been, but she still knew how to ride. And she'd get better at it. But Pesah couldn't ride a horse. There was no way. How was she supposed to get him to Byzantium? Push his chair all the way there?

How was Uncle Sabriel planning on doing it? He always came by himself on horseback, unless he was bringing something large. And then he arrived in his own red wagon.

Ziva's family had a red wagon. It was neglected, but she knew the servants still kept it in working order. Before Pesah had gotten really sick, Baba had loaded all of them into it from time to time and driven it around the city. Just for fun. Ziva liked to sit on the bench up front with him, taking turns smacking the horses' flanks with the long reins.

She knew where the wagon was. And she knew where the horses were. And she could probably figure out how to hook the horses into their traces. Right?

Ziva changed out of her nightgown and into her plainest kaftan and her most comfortable boots. She piled a bunch more clothes and wrapped them up in her bedsheet, tying the bundle so she could carry it. Her mother had gotten Ziva some small trinkets and jewelry, which Ziva never wore, but now she grabbed them and stuck them in her pockets. They were real gold, real silver, real gems. She could sell them, or trade them to a Byzantine doctor as payment.

Ziva peered into the hallway. No one was around, so she hurried out toward the stables where the horses and the disused wagon were kept.

THIRTEEN

THE STABLES WERE EMPTY of stable hands or grooms or any other servants that would normally have been there. The horses had all been brushed and put away, and they turned their lazy heads toward Ziva as she rushed past them to the red wagon. She climbed up on the wagon, throwing her bundle of clothes in the back. It wasn't even dusty; the servants kept it clean and ready to go, even though it had been years since the family had used it.

The reins and traces were attached to a long wooden piece jutting from the front of the wagon. All the leather pieces were well-oiled and soft. Ziva paced the stables, considering which horses to bring. The wagon was set up for two. Which two were the fastest? Did they get along? If she chose the wrong two horses, would they fight instead of pull the wagon?

She came to a stop in the aisle between stalls. She needed to bring food for them. What if they traveled somewhere without grass? Should she just fill the back of the wagon with hay?

The sun was setting and the stables were darkening fast. She had to hurry.

Ziva packed half of the wagon with hay. It was covered, so she didn't have to worry about any of it blowing away. But the wagon wasn't meant for hauling hay. It was meant for living inside. Regardless, she covered up the sleeping mats and the built-in chests and the little porthole window in one side, stacking the hay to the ceiling. She left enough room for her and Pesah to lie down when it was time to sleep. She also packed a couple blankets for the horses, in case it got cold.

Ziva picked the two horses whose stalls were closest to the wagon. Their coats were both rich brown, but one had a white face and the other didn't. The one with the white face came first, and stood still while she hitched him into the traces. He balked some at the bit going in his mouth, but didn't fight it too much. The second horse was a little more excitable, and she kept pawing at the ground with a hoof while Ziva hitched her in. She tossed her head when Ziva tried to put the bit in her mouth, but eventually allowed it.

Ziva checked and double-checked and triple-checked the traces, making sure all the buckles were tight and there were no loose connections anywhere. When she was satisfied that she'd done it properly, and the horses hadn't started nipping at one another at all, she slipped out of the stables and ran to Pesah's house.

No one was around. Pesah was alone. Ziva frowned in the darkness and told herself that when they returned and Pesah was cured, everyone in this house would have a *lot* of apologizing to do.

Inside, Pesah was in bed. But he wasn't asleep. As soon as Ziva was through the doorway, Pesah said, "You're not supposed to be here."

Ziva snorted and rummaged in Pesah's closet for an extra bedsheet. Like she had with her own sheet, she packed Pesah's with extra clothes, plus gauze and linen and even some of his books on top for if he got bored.

Pesah watched her silently for a while and then said, "Why are you stealing my things?"

"I'm not," Ziva said. "We're running away."

"We are?"

"Yes."

"To where?" Pesah said. "Samkarsh?"

"Byzantium," Ziva said.

Pesah coughed for a few moments, then cleared his throat. "What's in Byzantium?"

"Doctors." Ziva pushed his chair to the bedside and said, "Get in. Hurry."

"I'm in my pajamas," he said.

"You can change later," Ziva said, "when we're away from here."

Pesah didn't move to get into the chair. "If what Baba said is true . . . Sabriel thinks I can make you sick. What if that's true?"

"It's not," Ziva said. "I'm fine. Get in your chair. We have to hurry."

"But what if it is?"

"Then whoever cures you in Byzantium can cure me too," Ziva said. "Pesah, I am *not* going to let you die. I'll fight the Angel of Death itself for you. You said it has a lot of eyes? Well, I'll poke all its eyes out."

To Ziva's surprise, Pesah burst into laughter, which made her start laughing. Even though she was serious. She'd jab the Angel of Death in every single one of its eyeballs if that meant keeping Pesah safe.

Finally, the twins stopped laughing, and Pesah said, "Do you really think there's a cure in Byzantium?"

"We won't know until we get there," Ziva said.

And she helped Pesah get into the chair. She set the bundle of clothes and wound dressings on his lap, and she pushed him as quickly as she dared across the property to the stables. They passed a few servants but none of them said anything.

In the stables, Ziva helped Pesah into the back of the wagon, secured his wheeled chair and his belongings, and latched the back door of the wagon. Then she opened the stable doors wide before hopping onto the wagon bench and grabbing up the reins.

She paused. Heart thumping behind her ribs. Breaths coming fast and shallow.

"Is this stupid?" Ziva whispered out loud. Maybe it was. Stealing her family's old wagon, which she didn't know how to drive, and running away to Byzantium, which she didn't know how to get to, so Pesah could be cured by a doctor there, which she didn't know was even possible.

But what was the alternative?

Letting Pesah be neglected.

Letting Pesah be taken away.

Letting Pesah die.

He's going to die anyway.

She shook her head, getting Baba's voice out of there. The stable doors were open and the night waited outside, deep and dark.

Darkness. Ziva hated how it swallowed and obscured. But Pesah was with her. The darkness didn't scare her as long as he was there.

She slapped the reins on the horses' flanks, and they pulled the old red wagon out of the stables and into the night.

PART TWO

So Ziva and Pesah ran away from home! Ziva was so desperate to save her brother from *malach ha-mavet*, she was willing to risk the fury of her father, the rabbi, even the Khagan and the Bek, to do it.

Would you do something like this for someone you love?

You nod. Of course, of course. And I believe you. I've seen some amazing things done in the name of love.

But in this case, will it be enough?

They went west first, and then south. Ziva drove the wagon tirelessly, afraid to stop in case her father had sent men after them, to take them back to Atil. Always watchful for Uncle Sabriel, in case he decided to make the trip to Atil early. On and on she went, until finally she couldn't keep her eyes open a moment longer.

And that's when the demon found her.

FOURTEEN

ZIVA WOKE TO gruff voices nearby.

At first, she couldn't remember where she was. There was hay all around her, and Pesah's chair, and . . .

"Pesah?" Ziva mumbled, sitting up, rubbing an eye.

Pesah sat beside her, eyes wide, and before she could ask him anything he put a finger across his mouth. "Shh!"

She obeyed, and they listened to someone speaking outside the wagon. The men's words were too low for Ziva to make out, but it was clear that they were circling the wagon. Ziva watched the inside of the wagon, tracking the voices until they arrived at the back of the wagon, where the door was.

The door shifted as someone pulled on it from the outside.

She had locked the door last night before collapsing. The lock held as whoever was outside tried to open the door, gently at first, then harder as he realized that it wasn't opening easily.

Ziva didn't know how sturdy the lock was. Would it hold against someone who really, really wanted inside?

She wasn't going to sit there and wait to see.

As quietly as she could, she got up and crept toward the front of the wagon. A little sliding door there would let her out onto the bench, and since she'd left the horses in their traces last night, she'd be able to just grab the reins and get out of there.

Pesah watched her, saying nothing.

Ziva slid the door open a tiny bit, checking for anyone in front of the wagon. She saw no one, and the horses were still in their traces, so she threw the sliding door open and pulled herself onto the bench, grabbing the reins and slapping them against the horses' flanks as she shouted, "Hyah!"

Both horses jumped and bolted, startled by the sudden instruction to go. Ziva heard a man shout behind her, but it didn't stop her from slapping the reins again to urge the horses to go faster. They did, and Ziva was silently celebrating her escape when a boy dropped from the top of the wagon onto the bench.

His sudden appearance made her yelp and pull away. She couldn't tell much about him; he had a balaclava over his face, and all she could see were his dark eyes. He lunged for the reins in her hands.

"No!" Ziva yelled, transferring the reins to her far hand and using the closer one to whack at him.

He said nothing, just fended off her blows with a fore-
arm while still reaching for the reins. He was taller than her
and had a longer reach, and Ziva yelped as he pulled the
reins out of her hand.

"Give those back!" she demanded.

He said nothing. Just pulled the reins. Pulled the horses
to a stop.

Ziva shoved him sideways with all her might. He let out
a surprised cry and very nearly tumbled off the side, but
managed to grab her shoving arm and steady himself. He
let up on the horses' reins, and when Ziva saw them slack,
she shouted, "Hyah!"

Even in the absence of reins slapping their flanks, the
horses moved forward, pulling the wagon along the road
again.

Before the boy could pull them to a stop again, Ziva
struck at the boy's face, hoping to break his nose like she
had Reuven's, but he dodged her well enough to miss
the bulk of her blow. She opened her hand as it passed his
face, grabbing his balaclava with her fingers. She ripped
it up, pulling it over his eyes, enough for him to be unable
to see.

Then she grabbed the reins out of his hands, leaned
away, and set her feet against his side. She shoved now with
her legs instead of her arms, and sent him flying off the
bench.

Almost.

He hung onto the side, and Ziva growled, "Go away, already!"

The balaclava was still up over his eyes, and he used one arm to hold himself on the side of the wagon and the other to pull the balaclava off. He was young, like her, but haggard, like he hadn't slept or eaten well for years. A long scar slashed across his face from his left cheek down to where it curled under his chin and down his throat. His dark eyes met hers, and in that moment, a cold shudder spread out from her core, deadening her arms and legs and mind. She couldn't move.

His eyes flashed, catching the sunlight and something else, and the horses started to slow.

Ziva didn't try to get them running again. She wanted to, she just *couldn't move.* She stared at the boy as he climbed back onto the bench. He sat beside her, taking the reins from her limp hands, and he sighed.

"Sorry," he said as rapid footsteps approached the wagon, and he sounded like he meant it.

Two large men arrived around the side of the wagon with long knives drawn, and one of them snapped, "What took you so long?"

The boy beside Ziva said, "Little complication. Nothing serious."

The second man, who was taller than the first with a bald head, sneered at Ziva and said, "Little is right. How old are you, Princess?"

Ziva couldn't answer. She heard what they said, but no matter how hard she tried, she couldn't muster up words or movement or . . . anything. What had the boy done to her? Was he some kind of magician?

The two men didn't wait for Ziva to answer. One of them pointed a dirty thumb at her and said, "Put her in the back. We'll take the wagon to camp and see what's inside."

No! Ziva wanted to scream it but she couldn't make her mouth move. She just sat there, helpless. Useless.

The boy nodded and slid the door into the wagon open. "We'll go to the back."

She crawled through the door as though someone else was moving her body. She sat on the floor next to Pesah, who said, "Ziva?"

He stopped when the boy slipped through the door. The boy stopped too, looking surprised. The two of them stared at one another for a moment, and Ziva wondered if the boy was using the same trick on Pesah that he'd done to her.

"Who are you?" Pesah asked. The boy had not used his trick, then, for whatever reason.

The boy slid the door shut behind him and sat across from Ziva and Pesah. The wagon started to move again before he said, "My name is Almas. And I'm sorry. I'm really, really sorry."

FIFTEEN

"EXCUSE ME?" PESAH ASKED in his soft way. "What are you sorry for?"

Almas didn't answer for a while, and when Ziva wasn't sure he ever would, he answered with a question of his own: "Where are your parents?"

Ziva bristled, but trapped as she was inside herself, she couldn't tell him to mind his own business. She knew Pesah would never say that.

Pesah answered back, with another question. "Where are yours?"

Almas narrowed his eyes. He had dark hair, messy and curling at the nape of his neck, matted down from the balaclava. Ziva's eyes went back to the scar down his face and throat, wondering what kind of thing could do that to someone and not kill them.

"How do you know they're not my parents?" Almas said, nodding toward the front of the wagon where the two men sat on the bench outside.

Pesah shrugged stiffly. "So robbery is the family business, then?"

Almas was silent for a second, and then laughed. "Maybe."

Ziva couldn't crow out loud that Pesah had won their question conversation by making Almas respond with a statement, but she did it in her head.

Almas and Pesah regarded one another for a few breaths, and then Almas said, "I've seen people like you in the cities. They're made to wear bells."

Pesah withdrew his bandaged hands to his lap. "Bells?"

"So people can hear them coming," Almas said, "and stay away from them."

Pesah nodded, looking down. Ziva wanted to hug him, and then slap Almas.

"I don't have to wear bells," Pesah said softly.

"No," Almas said. "They're all beggars. You're not a beggar. Would your family pay money to get you back?"

Pesah glanced at Ziva, eyes like an overcast sky. *Would* their parents pay to get Pesah back? Of course they would, Ziva thought angrily, but not with all of her heart.

"Why aren't you saying anything, Ziva?" Pesah asked her. When she didn't reply, he looked at Almas. "What's wrong with her?"

Almas glanced at Ziva, and his eyes flashed again. "Nothing," he said, and the coldness that had been keeping her motionless thawed away.

Ziva's mouth opened and she snapped, "He cursed me!"

Almas laughed. "Cursed? What am I, a witch?"

"Maybe!" Ziva snarled, lunging for the boy. She was about to give him another scar to complement the one he had. He barely dodged her swiping hand in time. "It's none of your business where our parents are, and none of your business to talk to him like that."

Almas caught her wrist as she tried to smack him again. "Stop!"

"Then let us go!" Ziva wrenched her wrist away from him and made for the back door.

Almas was there then, blocking her, arms splayed out.

"I can't!" Almas said, moving to block her whenever she tried to dodge around him. "And what's your plan anyway? Jump out of the moving wagon? And go where? We're in the middle of nowhere."

Ziva jammed her fists on her hips. "And you think if we go with you, it'll be better for us than jumping out?"

Almas hesitated. "Maybe."

"We need to go to Constantinople!" Ziva said, pointing at Pesah. "He's sick. We need to get him to a doctor who can help him."

Almas looked at Pesah with a raised eyebrow, and then looked back at Ziva. In a low voice, he said, "There are no doctors who can help him."

Ziva extended a finger and jabbed Almas in the chest with it. He was bonier than she expected; the tip of her finger throbbed from the hardness of his bone under skin. "You're just some honorless thug. What do you know about anything?"

Almas ground his teeth together. "I know the men out front want money over anything else, and if they think you can get them some, they won't kill you. And if you're too much trouble . . ." He swallowed hard, and the scar on his face and neck seemed to stand out more. "Just don't be trouble."

From his spot on the floor, Pesah said, "We won't be trouble. Right, Ziva?"

Ziva was ready to cause as much trouble as possible, but when Pesah turned his pleading eyes on her, she sighed. "Fine." She turned to Almas again. "We won't get hurt if we cooperate?"

Almas shook his head. "No. Avag and Petros are thieves. They're not murderers."

"*They?*" Ziva said. "I think you mean *we.*"

"I meant what I said," Almas muttered, and he sat in front of the back door, arms crossed.

Ziva returned to Pesah, and after a moment, she grabbed her bundled sheet with her possessions inside. Casting furtive glances at Almas, who seemed to be too busy brooding to notice her, she grabbed the jewelry she had stashed in the bag. Those thieves could take the horses and the wagon and their clothes, but she was going to keep the jewelry. Some of it, at least. She turned away from Almas so he couldn't see what she was doing, and unlaced her boot.

Pesah whispered, "What are you doing?"

"We still need something to pay the doctors in Constantinople," she said. She looped the gold chain of her most expensive necklace around her ankle, then pulled her stocking over it. "I'm not going to let those jerks take it."

Pesah frowned under his wrappings. "You still want to go to Byzantium?"

"Of course!" Ziva hissed. "Someone there has a cure, Pesah. I know it."

He watched her pull her boot back on, and said, "No trouble, Ziva."

"I know, I know." She tucked her re-booted foot under her. The chain pressed into her skin reassuringly. She glanced down at her iron date palm brooch, wondering if the thieves would care about iron. They might care about the purple gems. So she took the brooch off and pinned it to the underside of her kaftan's bottom hem, where the thieves hopefully wouldn't notice it. "We'll get away somehow."

Neither of them said anything for a while. Almas stared away, like Pesah and Ziva weren't even there. The thieves on the bench outside laughed and made vulgar jokes. Ziva tried not to listen.

Then the wagon slowed, and stopped. The wagon shifted as the men got off the bench, and Pesah grabbed Ziva's hand.

"What if they take my chair?" Pesah asked.

"Then I guess I'll have to carry you to Byzantium," Ziva said, and Pesah sighed out a short laugh that was cut off when the back of the wagon opened and the two thieves stood there, grinning.

"Welcome home," one of them said. "Now, let's see what you're worth."

SIXTEEN

THEY WEREN'T WORTH A LOT, apparently. They stood to the side as the thieves ransacked the wagon. They wouldn't give Pesah his chair, so Ziva had to hold him up. As she waited for the thieves to rip their wagon apart, Ziva looked around their new location. They were in an open space surrounded on all sides by rock, like this place had been a cavern once but had gotten its top sliced off. The walls of the old cavern had been worn away a lot, and a big tree stood on one side of the rock clearing. There was a little bubbling spring near that tree. Two other wagons, similar to Ziva's but unpainted and in disrepair, sat side by side near the tree; a distance away from the center of the clearing, there was a fire pit full of half-burned wood.

The ground was rocky and uneven. Even if Ziva got Pesah's chair, she'd break the wheels on the rocks if she tried to escape with him.

No. She'd have to be patient. Escape at night, while the thieves were sleeping or otherwise occupied.

The thieves threw all their things out of the wagon and then charged at Ziva and Pesah as they stood by their scattered belongings.

"Is this it?" the taller, balder one roared, holding a handful of the jewelry Ziva had intended to pay a Byzantine doctor with.

Ziva winced away. He smelled bad, and he was loud, and he seemed angry. Almas had called them Avag and Petros, and she wondered who this stinky one was. She found herself seeking Almas, who stood apart from the group, next to the horses. He had one by the harness and was patting her nose. He wouldn't look at Ziva.

Then a hand grabbed her chin, turning her gaze to the shorter of the thieves. He snarled, "Petros asked you a question. Answer him!"

Oh. This was Avag, then. *Just don't be trouble,* Almas had said. Ziva couldn't believe she was going to be cordial to these jerks. She balled her hands into fists and breathed in deep.

She nodded. "That's it."

Avag didn't let go of her like she'd hoped. He instead turned her head side to side, inspecting her. "How much would you fetch us, huh?"

Her lips pressed against one another and she felt her nostrils flare. "My parents will pay a lot to get us back." She pointed to herself and then Pesah.

Avag just then seemed to notice Pesah's bandages. He let go of Ziva's face and, without warning, yanked down the bandage over Pesah's mouth and cheeks.

Pesah and Avag recoiled at the same time, and Ziva scrambled to pull Pesah's bandages back up.

"A leper!" Avag spat as he scrambled back. He wiped his hand off on his dirty pants.

Ziva clenched her teeth. "So? He's not going to hurt you!"

Avag kept wiping his hand. "You said your parents would pay to get you back. Maybe *you*. But not *him*."

Pesah's next inhalation was shaky, and Ziva snarled, "What would *you* know? You're just a stupid thief!"

Avag's face darkened, and he pointed a dirty finger at Ziva. "Watch your mouth, girl."

"Ziva," Pesah said softly. "No trouble."

Don't be trouble. That's what Almas had said, but Almas was working with these guys. Maybe he'd told her not to be trouble to make the kidnapping easier.

Ziva said, "Send a message to my parents in Atil. They'll pay. For *both of us*."

Avag sneered. "Not even a mother could love a face like that." He jabbed a dirty finger at Pesah, who recoiled away.

"Our mother does so love him!" Ziva barked, then fell quiet, startled by the conviction of her own words. Their mother loved Pesah. Of course she did—at least *some*. Maybe not enough to give him a birthday party, but definitely enough to pay a ransom to get him back from thieves. "Send a message! You'll see!"

Avag glared at her for a minute, and then he turned to look at Almas. He snapped his fingers in Almas's direction. "C'mere."

Almas came, slipping over like a beaten dog, eyes downcast. Avag grabbed Almas by the arm and said, "They got anything valuable?"

With big, regretful eyes, Almas looked up at Ziva. He didn't say yes or no or anything, and Ziva's ankle throbbed where the necklace was hidden.

"Answer me!" Avag barked, and Almas jumped, winced. And nodded.

The short thief grinned at Ziva. "Oh yeah? What is it?"

Almas sighed heavily. "A necklace."

Ziva's mouth dropped open, and she snapped it shut as fast as she could. She pointed to her throat and said, "You liar. I don't have a necklace."

Avag looked at Almas, eyebrows raised.

Almas pointed at Ziva's feet. "She hid it in her boot."

Avag cackled, and Ziva glowered at Almas. "Why would I hide a necklace in my boot?"

"Anything else?" Avag asked.

Almas blew a slow breath out. "And there's a brooch under the bottom hem of her kaftan."

Ziva's mouth dropped open, and she tried to recover by yelling, "You liar!"

Petros appeared from inside Ziva's wagon, cracking his knuckles, and Avag said to Almas, "Take the sick one away."

Ziva grabbed Pesah's arm as Almas came closer. He continued to look regretful, but that didn't stop Ziva from shoving him when he reached for Pesah.

"Don't touch him," Ziva growled.

"I have to," Almas whispered.

Ziva put herself between Almas and Pesah, but the thief boy just pushed her sideways, out of the way, and as soon as she was out of Pesah's reach, Petros grabbed her by the arm.

"Let go of me!" Ziva screamed, clawing at Petros's hand. "They'll pay for both of us!" She watched Almas hold Pesah up as the pair walked away, and Pesah cast Ziva a backwards glance.

Avag grabbed Ziva's face again, pointing it at his own. "Will they pay enough to make him worth keeping around? I don't think so, Princess. They might even reward us for culling him for them."

Ziva snarled and swung at Avag with her free hand, and she caught the side of his head with her open palm. Avag grabbed her wrist, ripped it away, and then slapped her hard across the face.

Ziva covered her slapped skin with a trembling hand, tears pricking and burning in her eyes. Avag leveled a finger at her face and said, "There's more where that came from. Maybe I'll break your nose next time. Your parents won't care if you've got a broken nose, will they? I don't think so. Now gimme that jewelry."

Ziva blinked her tears away. "No."

Avag swung his hand up and Ziva winced away.

But he didn't hit her.

When she looked up next, he laughed in her face, and Petros laughed from behind her. Then Avag ducked down to Ziva's feet and tore her boots off. She tried to kick at him, but he held her legs, and crowed when he found her hidden necklace, tearing it away from her. Then he pulled the palm tree brooch out from where she'd pinned it under her kaftan.

"Tie her up at my wagon," Avag said to Petros, and he pinned Ziva's brooch to his shirt with a cackle as Petros dragged Ziva away.

SEVENTEEN

ZIVA STIFFENED HER LIP. She was *not* going to cry. No. Definitely not.

She'd thought Almas was okay. She had been wrong.

Almas had tied Pesah to the tree on the outskirts of the camp, and Pesah had gone without a fight. Ziva wanted to fight for him, but she was chained up to the wagon.

Nearby, Avag and Petros talked back and forth, arguing in low voices. Ziva could make out bits of the conversation, but not enough to figure out what they were really talking about.

No matter what she did, she couldn't slip her hands out of the shackles. Every time she tried to escape from the shackles, the pale spot on her wrist caught her eye again. She tried rubbing it off. No change. No feeling.

Then she heard another voice from behind her: "Hey."

She spun, scowling. Almas stood around the wagon's corner, peering out. Ziva charged at him, but her shackles were too short, so she couldn't reach him.

He watched her try to grab for him and then let her arms drop to her sides. "They're going to leave him to die there."

"Yeah," Ziva spat, her throat tightening. "Thanks so much for helping them!"

"I had to," he said softly.

Ziva didn't want to scream at him, because she didn't want Avag and Petros to notice their conversation. So she hissed through clenched teeth, "You keep saying that. Why do you have to?"

"I want to help," he said.

"Then help!"

"First, I need you to do something for me."

Ziva gaped at him. She couldn't believe he was trying to bargain after he'd betrayed her and Pesah so many times. She didn't know what to say, so she opted to do what Baba would have done: stay silent.

Almas waited for her to speak, his eyebrows creeping up his forehead more with every passing moment of silence. Finally, he said, "Can you?"

She said nothing.

Almas waited another handful of seconds, then said, "It's easy. I need you to break a bowl. That's all."

Ziva was silent, even though she had a million questions to ask him about such a weird request.

Almas sounded frustrated when he said, "Are you going to say anything?"

"Sure," she said after a pause. "Did you just ask me to break some pottery for you?"

"One very specific bowl," Almas said. "I even know where Avag keeps it."

"Why?"

"Because," he said, "I need it to be broken."

"And you can't break it yourself?" Ziva asked.

Almas sighed, frustrated, and said, "No. It's, um, like a loyalty thing. You or Pesah have to break it to prove to me you're on my side."

A long time ago, Baba had told Ziva that an Important Skill judges must learn is to tell when someone was lying. He had shown her some tells: shifting eyes, crossing arms, and halting speech. Almas was doing all three of those things. He was lying. But why would he lie about breaking a bowl?

Ziva said, "If I break that bowl, you'll help me and Pesah?"

Almas nodded. "To the fullest of my ability."

And he extended his hand.

Ziva stared at it. His hand was dirty, his fingernails chewed to stubs. The hand of a thief, and who knew what else. If she helped him, what kind of trouble was she getting herself into?

But if she didn't help him, and he didn't help her . . . she might die, and Pesah certainly would.

So Ziva reached out and clasped Almas's hand in her own. They shook three times, and each time their hold became heavier and heavier, until on the third time she could hardly muster the strength to lift her arm. Then Almas let go, and the heaviness was gone.

"Where's the bowl?" Ziva asked.

He pointed. "Inside the wagon you're chained to. It's shallow and wide." He made an approximation of its size. "Just plain clay. It has a bunch of symbols carved into it."

"What do the symbols mean?" Ziva asked.

Almas scowled. "Who cares?"

"I want to know what I'm breaking!" Ziva said.

"It's an old poem or something," Almas said. "It doesn't matter. Break it. You can just throw it against the ground. It'll shatter. Then get ready to run."

"Wait," Ziva said. "Now?"

"Yes." Almas took out a key and inserted it into the shackle keyhole. He twisted, and the shackles loosened around Ziva's wrists. "Now."

"Why now?" Ziva said, rubbing the skin that had been under the shackles. "I'm not prepared. I need to pack an escape bag or—"

"It has to be now," Almas said. "Go find it. Hurry."

Ziva narrowed her eyes, ready to call off this whole thing, but then she remembered the handshake. That was binding, wasn't it? Even to a thief? She'd show her loyalty and then he'd show his, and they could get out of here and back on the road to Byzantium.

Ziva glanced around the side of the wagon. Avag and Petros were no longer arguing back and forth, so Ziva turned back to Almas.

"Hey, can you distract them or—"

But he was gone. She was talking to no one.

"Figures," Ziva grumbled, and turned again. Both men seemed busy doing something or other by the fire, so Ziva crept up to the side of the wagon, cracked the door open, and peered in.

It was dark inside, but even in the sliver of light that fell across the floor from the door's small opening, she could tell it was full of junk and clutter. It smelled just as bad as Avag did. She glanced back at the men at the fire, held her breath, and ducked inside the wagon. She propped the door open a tiny bit with a piece of junk so she could see. She sifted through a pile of dirty dishes, but didn't find any bowls with carvings. So she checked under some dirty clothes, behind the bed and benches, inside chests and boxes, and—

Someone shouted outside: "She's gone!"

Oh no.

Ziva rummaged faster. Where was this stupid bowl? Was it even a real thing? She started to think about all the reasons Almas had to set her up. The same reason he'd told on her for hiding the jewelry? The same reason he'd stood by and hadn't said anything when Avag had hit her?

There were drawers under the bed that she hadn't pulled out yet, so she did. One had only some old food with ants on it, and she slammed it shut as she grimaced. She pulled the next drawer open.

And there it was.

A bowl as Almas had described, with words she couldn't make out inscribed in a spiral inside and outside the bowl. At the very bottom of the inside, someone had carved a demonic figure with bird's feet and protruding fangs.

As Ziva picked the bowl up, the wagon door opened. Avag stood there, staring at her in horror, the purple gems of the palm tree brooch flashing from where it was pinned to his shirt.

"What are you doing?" he yelled, and pulled himself into the wagon.

Ziva held the bowl over her head, and Avag screamed as she threw it against the floor with all her might.

EIGHTEEN

THE BOWL EXPLODED APART, shards flying out in every direction. One hit her wrist and made a tiny cut, and another did the same to her cheek.

"You stupid girl!" Avag grabbed her by the front of her kaftan and ripped her off her feet. His voice boomed in her face, foul breath blasting all around her. "You've doomed us all!"

She didn't have time to ask how breaking a bowl had doomed anyone, because Avag was pulled away from her. *Torn* away from her. And flung out the back of the wagon. He skidded across the rocky ground and came to a stop near a horrified Petros.

Almas was standing at the back of the wagon. When he turned to Ziva, he looked the same as he had every other time she'd seen him. But off. Just a little. She couldn't figure out how.

"Thank you," Almas said to her, and he turned to face Avag and Petros. He strode across the camp, closing the distance with impossibly long strides, and seized Avag by the throat. Petros turned and ran.

Ziva dashed out of the wagon, grabbing Pesah's chair on the way, and ran to her brother, who was watching the events in the camp with rapt horror. Their horses had been returned to their wagon, and the wagon waited near the tree Pesah was tied to. Had Almas done that? She didn't have time to wonder. She untied him and said, "We have to run, Pesah."

"What's happening?" Pesah asked.

"I don't know," Ziva said, even though she thought maybe she did. A little. But that was impossible.

Someone screamed from behind them, and Ziva turned. Petros had fallen backwards, scrambling away from . . . something. Ziva couldn't see it very well. It threw a long shadow on the ground, falling over Petros as he tried to get away. It looked like a man, but—

Wings.

It had wings. Six of them. And eyes that blinked and rolled within the shadow itself, as though they had punched holes in it.

And a sword that cast a shadow that hissed and burned across the ground.

Ziva couldn't move. She was frozen, staring . . . just like she'd been when Almas had taken control of the wagon.

Then Pesah grabbed her wrist and breathed out, *"Malach ha-mavet."*

His touch broke whatever had frozen her in place, and Ziva hauled him to his feet. She supported him as he hobbled in the opposite direction of the creature and the screaming thieves. To their wagon, where she helped him climb into the back and then shut the door behind him.

When she went back for the chair, the winged shadow was closer. And somehow she knew—she wasn't sure how, but somehow she knew—*malach ha-mavet* was looking at her.

Then the winged shadow was gone, and four dark figures on horses rode into the camp. They came fast, swords up, horse hooves thundering across the ground.

Almas stood where the Angel of Death's shadow had been, and behind him the men on horseback circled the screaming Avag and Petros, swords flashing, slashing, red.

Almas took a step toward her, and Ziva turned. She left the chair. She scrambled onto the bench and yelled, "Hyah!" before she was even seated. The reins nearly fell away from her as the horses lurched forward, but she caught them in time, smacking the horses' flanks fast, maybe too hard, panicking as she drove them away from the campsite and the death that swirled within it.

NINETEEN

THE PANIC IN ZIVA'S CHEST kept her awake so she could drive the horses all night, and her mind swirled with a million different thoughts. Once upon a time, she'd heard stories in the synagogue about angels. Sometimes they could appear as people, right? But nowhere in her education had it ever been mentioned that angels could be held captive inside a bowl.

That was what she'd just seen, wasn't it?

Almas was an angel. Maybe he was even the Angel of Death itself. And those thieves had been holding him hostage with the bowl Ziva had shattered.

No. She shook her head, both against her fatigue and against the thought that two dirty thieves could enslave the Angel of Death. That was impossible.

Right?

Or was it?

It was also impossible that she had just seen an angel with her own eyes and walked away without any trouble.

Angels were supposed to be *too much* for a person's eyes or mind to be able to comprehend. Even knowing their names was more than a mind could bear. She should have been blind and mad.

So what was Almas? And why had the Angel of Death been helping him?

Did the Angel of Death have assistants?

She shook her head again. That thought was completely ridiculous. Maybe she'd gone mad after all.

At daybreak, she finally slowed the horses. They came to a stop near a small stream, and after she checked the road behind to make sure no men with swords or Angel of Death or Almas were following, she checked on Pesah in the back.

He was asleep, curled up half on the hay, and Ziva left him there while she unhitched the horses to lead them to the stream to drink and eat some grass. As they did, she sat in the grass and rifled through her memories of synagogue for mention of the Angel of Death having assistants.

Ziva noticed a pebble in the grass that was flat and smooth, and out of habit she picked it up to inspect it. Another one was a reach away, so she shifted to grab it, and as she did she caught sight of that pale spot on her wrist. She stared at it, and then glanced at the wagon where Pesah slept. He had pale spots on him. And if she poked his, he said he couldn't feel anything.

Uncle Sabriel had told Baba that Pesah could make them sick. Make her sick.

She reached a finger over to press on the pale spot, and one of the horses wandered to her and snuffled at her hair. She left that pale spot for now and patted him. "I just want to get to Byzantium."

The horse sniffed her again and then returned to eating grass.

Ziva flopped back on the cool grass, pebbles held in a loose fist, letting the morning sun stream over her face. She knew she should get going again, but she was tired. She'd lie here for a moment. Just a moment. She shut her eyes and breathed in slowly. And then a shadow fell over her face. One of the horses, she thought, until a familiar voice said, "Oh good. I found you."

Ziva bolted upright, hands up. Almas stood over her, blocking out the sun, smiling. *Smiling.* She scrambled backwards, and he stood still with the horses still nibbling grass around him. Ziva thumped into the wagon as she retreated, and used it to get to her feet.

She leveled an accusatory finger at him. "Get away from me! I did your favor, now the least you can do is leave us alone!"

Almas beamed. He ambled toward her, looking more relaxed and happy than she had yet seen him. He was still very skinny, and he still sported the scar on his face, but he seemed like an entirely new person otherwise.

An *entirely* new person, because now she knew what he really was.

"Stay away from my brother!" Ziva screamed, and hucked the pebbles in her hand at him.

The pebbles flew at Almas's face, and he winced away from them. "Ow! What was that for?"

She didn't answer. Back in Atil, she'd told Pesah that she'd poke the Angel of Death in every one of its many eyes, and she'd meant it. Screaming, she went for Almas's face, and he let out a scream of his own as he ducked back and swatted her hands away.

"What are you *doing?*" Almas yelled.

Ziva continued to reach for his eyes. "You can't have him! I don't care if you're *malach ha-mavet!* I won't let you take him!"

"*Malach ha*—OW!" Almas grabbed her wrists, pulling her swiping fingernails away from his face. She'd gotten him across the cheek, leaving a pink line on his skin. "I'm not a *malach!*"

"Fine, you're its assistant!" Ziva accused him, tugging her wrists away from his hands. "Either way, leave Pesah alone!"

"Assistant?" Almas said, incredulous. "I'm not . . . *malachim* don't have assistants."

"Then what are you?" Ziva asked, leveling a finger at his face. "Don't lie to me. I know you're not a person!"

He hesitated, then said, "I *am* a person."

"People can't do the things you did," Ziva said. "Tell me the truth!"

He hesitated again, longer, shifting from foot to foot, and then he said, "I'm, um . . . a sheyd."

Ziva's stomach clenched, and every bit of moisture in her mouth evaporated. A sheyd. At the synagogue, she'd heard a story about sheydim. Demons. They could be bound to objects by powerful rabbis to keep them under control.

Could they be bound to bowls?

Ziva's mother had spoken of sheydim too, and mazzikim. Haunting nighttime places, waiting to harm people and trick them into making bad choices. The way her mother spoke of sheydim, Ziva had imagined them to be absolutely everywhere, packing every inch of space possible.

Maybe they were, and were just invisible.

Maybe her mother had exaggerated a little.

Ziva always thought of sheydim as things that had existed more a thousand years ago, and had gone away before her time. She'd never seen a sheyd, or heard of anyone who had.

He had tricked her. The moment she'd broken the bowl, pandemonium had erupted. If he was a sheyd bound to that bowl, it would make sense. She had freed him. And he had killed Avag and Petros.

Almas's voice interrupted her panicking thoughts with: "Well, I'm not a full sheyd. Just half. My mother—"

"I don't care about your family history." Ziva pointed a stiff, trembling finger down the road. "Go away. I never want to see you again."

Almas lingered. He looked normal, but she knew he wasn't. Full sheyd or half sheyd . . . it didn't matter. Either way, he couldn't be trusted.

He shook his head. "I can't."

"Why not?"

"We have a deal," he said. "We shook on it."

Ziva shook her head. "No. You broke the deal when you lied to me, and killed those men. Deal off. Deal cancelled."

Almas's eyes grew wide. "Killed who?"

"Avag and Petros!" Ziva snapped. "Don't play stupid. I *saw* you."

"I didn't kill them."

"Then who did?" Ziva scowled. "You threw Avag across the camp and I saw you grab his throat."

Almas looked down at his hands. "I mean . . . I was really angry. Wouldn't you be? They kept me like a slave. Made me do things I didn't want to do. All that stuff I did to you and Pesah, I didn't want to do that. They made me."

"And now you're free," Ziva said, "and you can do all kinds of terrible things on your own. So I want you to go away."

He looked genuinely crestfallen. "Why do you think I'll do terrible things still?"

Ziva couldn't believe it. She yelled, "Because *you're a sheyd!* Your whole purpose is to be terrible!"

Almas's shoulders slumped. He looked equal parts angry and dejected. "You don't know anything," he muttered.

"I know I don't want you near me or my brother," Ziva said.

Almas scowled. "Well, that's not how this works. We made a deal, and neither of us can break it now. You already did your part, and I'm bound to do mine."

"I already said you don't have to," Ziva said. "I release you, or whatever. What do I have to say?"

"Nothing," Almas said. "You can't release me. It's done. The deal is set in stone. I'll have to follow you for the rest of our lives until I do what I said I would."

He looked just as unhappy about it as Ziva felt.

She sighed. "What did you say you'd do?"

"Help you and Pesah as much as I can," he said.

"So you can get us to Byzantium?" Ziva asked.

Almas hesitated before saying, "Yes, but I don't think that's where we need to go."

"You *said* you'd help!"

"I know!" Almas snapped. "But I don't think Byzantium will help. I said no one there can cure him, and I really think that's true, so taking you there won't help."

"Then where *should* we go?" Ziva asked. "How can you help us?"

Almas glanced around. "Last night. *Malach ha-mavet,*" he whispered, like saying the name too loud would summon the creature. "He was there so fast. Like he was already on the way." His eyes wandered to the wagon where Pesah slumbered. "I think the Angel of Death is following you, because . . ." He shifted from foot to foot. "Well, Pesah is dying."

"Shut up," Ziva said in a low voice.

"Denying it won't make it go away," Almas said.

"He isn't dying." Ziva's face felt hot, her hands tingled, and she was moments away from taking a swing at Almas again. "I'm going to save him."

Almas nodded carefully. "I know a place he'll be safe from the Angel of Death."

Ziva crossed her arms. "How is that even possible?"

"There's one place," Almas said. "A city to the east, in the Blue Lands. The Angel of Death isn't allowed within the walls, so no one there can die. If we take Pesah—"

"—then we can save him," Ziva finished, letting her arms drop to her sides. She narrowed her eyes. "This is a real place?"

"It's as real as sheydim are," Almas said, grinning.

Ziva didn't grin with him. "And you know how to get there?"

"I know what the legends say," Almas said. "I know the landmarks. We can find it."

Ziva nodded. "And as soon as you get us there, you'll leave us alone?"

Almas's grin fell off his face. "At that point, the deal will be done. I won't have a reason to be around you anymore. So yeah, I'll leave you alone."

"Fine," Ziva said.

Almas extended his hand. Another handshake. Ziva stared at it, glared at him, and then walked past him without touching or saying anything. She needed to get the horses hitched to the wagon again. She had a brother to save.

TWENTY

ALMAS HELPED ZIVA hitch the horses back up to the wagon, and then insisted he drive them so she could sleep. She narrowed her eyes suspiciously at him, and he scoffed.

"What do you think I'm going to do?" Almas asked. "Take you back to Avag and Petros?"

Well, he couldn't do that, right? They were dead. Unless he was threatening to kill her. Her eyes narrowed more.

"You've got to sleep sometime," Almas said. "I told you I'd help you, and I will. No tricks."

"No tricks?" she said. "You're a sheyd. Isn't it your job to play tricks on people?"

Almas's nostrils flared for a moment, and he said, "I'm half-sheyd. My always honest and never tricky human half will keep my wild sheyd half under control."

Ziva crossed her arms. "I'm not tired. I'll stay out here with you."

Almas sighed. "If you insist."

She did insist. She only trusted him as far as she could throw him. Which wasn't very far at all. They sat on the bench together and Almas took up the reins, coaxing the horses forward.

"We should only go half the day," he said. "The horses are tired. They need some rest."

"We need to get to that city," Ziva grumbled. The more time they wasted, the closer Pesah came to death . . . and also, the more likely it was that Baba would send someone to find them.

"We will," Almas said. "And we'll get there faster if we don't run the horses into the ground. At midday we'll find somewhere safe to let them rest. And you. You need to rest."

"I'll rest when Pesah's safe." How could she think to rest and relax when the Angel of Death was literally chasing Pesah down?

"It'll take us a couple weeks to get to the Blue Lands," Almas said.

Ziva thought of her gentle, brilliant brother slumbering in the back of the wagon. He didn't yet know that Almas was up here. Should she have woken him up and asked for his thoughts? She frowned, chest tightening, wondering if she had made a mistake in allowing Almas to come with them. "Then I'll rest in a couple weeks."

Almas scowled. "You don't have to be so stubborn all the time, you know."

"Says you," Ziva said. Sitting on the wagon with the cool morning breeze rustling her hair, feeling the rhythmic swaying of the wagon back and forth . . . it was lulling her to sleep. So she shifted, sat up straighter, and said, "Tell me what really happened last night."

Almas glanced at her sideways. "What?"

"What really happened," Ziva repeated. "You said you didn't kill Avag and Petros. But that's what it looked like to me. Explain."

Almas blew a long breath out. "Okay. Well. Um. What do you know about sheydim?"

That was a good question. She said, "I know what my rabbi has said. There are sheydim all around. They're responsible for lots of bad things. They, um . . . like if you go to open water at night, there's a sheyd that will make you blind. That kind of thing."

"That's Shabriri," Almas said.

Ziva snorted. "Of course you'd know its name. Is it your uncle or something?"

"No, we're not related. But I know about the other sheydim. Anyway, do you know what a sheyd is?"

"Something bad," Ziva said, arms crossed. What had Ziva's mother said about them? "A spirit of the evil inclination."

Almas was silent for a few moments. "Sheydim can be bad. Just like people can be bad. But no, that's not what I meant. I mean . . . you have *malachim*, the angels, and they do their thing. And you have people down here, doing their thing. And sheydim lie between. We have some things in common with people, and some things in common with angels."

Ziva rolled her eyes. "Oh, you have some things in common with angels?"

"Yes."

"Like what?"

Almas held up a hand and ticked the items off on his fingers: "We have wings. We can fly from one end of the earth to the other. And we can know the future."

Ziva made a show of leaning over and looking all around him, even though she was so tired her bones were thrumming. "Your wings must be very small."

"I don't have any," Almas snapped. "Because I'm only half-sheyd. Remember?"

"Does that mean you can't fly?"

"Yes," Almas said. "But I *can* hear the future."

"Hear it?" Ziva remembered the way Pesah's eyes had ticked all around the room during his vision, looking and looking. "Why hear and not see?"

Almas pondered for a moment, then said, "It's like standing on one side of a wall, and the people on the other side are having a secret conversation. But if you're still and you listen hard enough, you can understand what they're saying, or at least get an idea. I hear Hashem and the angels speaking of the future, and if I'm still and quiet, I can understand it, too."

They were both quiet while Ziva wrapped her mind around what he'd said. He could hear whispers of the future. Could he hear whispers of Pesah's death? She wanted to ask him, but she didn't want to let him know that Pesah had seen a vision. She couldn't trust a sheyd. Even a half sheyd. In Atil, things like sheydim and the Angel of Death were real, but they were real the way everything else heard in synagogue was real. They were things that had happened long ago, or happened to important people. Kings. Prophets. Not little girls and their sick brothers.

Although.

She thought of Pesah's vision. Was it a prophecy after all? But what did it mean if it was?

The lull in conversation was allowing her exhaustion to wrap itself around her. She searched her tired mind for something to say to keep the conversation going, but Almas spoke before she could.

"I heard the angels talking about Avag and Petros," he said. "Soldiers have been looking for them for a while. They were on their way to find them. To kill them."

Ziva blinked, exhaustion pulling at her. "Those horsemen."

Almas nodded. "I knew we needed to be gone before the soldiers got there. You never know with soldiers. Some of them are nice and good. Some of them are . . . not."

Ziva glanced at the scar on his face and throat, wanting to ask if soldiers had done that, but she didn't. That seemed very personal. Instead she asked, "Why did you care about us? To help us escape?"

Almas shrugged. "Because you helped me."

Ziva tilted her head down, looking at him through her brows. "There's more to it than that."

Almas watched the road for a few breaths. "Where I come from, kindness is enough." Then his eyes widened and he said, "Oh, I forgot." He reached into his kaftan's side pocket and pulled out something in his fist. He held it out to her, fingers obscuring the object.

Ziva regarded his fist suspiciously. "What is it?"

"Just take it."

She glared at him, and then held her hand, palm open, under his. He opened his fist, and her palm tree brooch dropped into her hand. The purple gems caught the sun and glittered, and Ziva's breath caught in her throat.

Almas said, "It seemed important to you. I thought you'd want it back."

Ziva pulled the brooch to her chest, clutching it in trembling fingers.

"I'm sorry I told them where it was," he said. "I had to. As long as that bowl was intact, I had to do whatever they said. But you broke it for me, so . . ." He shrugged. "I could make it right."

Ziva affixed the brooch to her kaftan in its usual place, comforted by the weight of it there. "Well, you definitely made it right."

Almas grinned. "See? Sheydim aren't so bad, are we?"

"I guess not." She pulled her crossed arms against her belly and leaned against the wagon. She blinked hard a few times. Her eyelids felt like they each weighed as much as a bucket full of water, and every blink was harder and harder to recover from.

"Almas," she said softly as she shut her eyes against the brightening sun. "Thank you."

She let her eyes shut now, and the last thing she heard before drifting off to sleep was Almas's voice: "You're welcome."

TWENTY-ONE

WHEN ZIVA WOKE UP, she was in the back of the wagon. Pesah and Almas were nowhere to be seen.

She sat up. There were voices outside the wagon. A lot of them. Like they were in a town marketplace. So Ziva opened the back door of the wagon and peered out.

The town was on the smaller side, certainly not a metropolis like Atil, but not tiny either. The marketplace was busy, and she wondered if Almas and Pesah had gone into it to get food. The thought of Pesah without his chair, wandering through the market, made Ziva's chest tight, and she hurried out of the wagon to find them.

"Ziva!" Pesah's voice from behind her. She turned, and saw his bandaged face peering out from the front of the wagon. He waved a hand at her, and she hurried over to him.

"Where's Almas?" she asked, and then groaned. "Oh. Um. I guess you know that Almas caught up to us, huh?"

Pesah nodded. "I figured it out when he brought you into the back of the wagon. He seems nice, for a sheyd."

Ziva's eyes widened. "How'd you know about that?"

"He told me."

"He did?"

Pesah nodded. "Yeah. And he asked if I was hungry, and that's why we stopped here."

Ziva faced the market. "So, he went in there?

"Yeah."

She glowered now. "And he just left you all by yourself?"

Pesah laughed. "You were here the whole time."

"I was asleep," Ziva argued.

"Well, that's fine though," Pesah said. "I was fine."

"But what if something had happened?" Ziva asked.

Pesah was quiet for a few breaths. "I'm not helpless, Ziva," he said in a tone that made her squint at him. He sounded irritated. Why was he irritated?

He must have been really hungry, or tired, or something. To change the subject, Ziva asked, "So he went to get food?"

Pesah nodded.

Ziva scrunched her face. "Does he have money?"

Pesah shrugged. "I don't know. I think so?" He sounded less irritated.

She glanced behind her, back into the market. "How long has he been gone?"

"A while," Pesah said. "I hope he's all right."

He was a sheyd. He'd used freeze magic on Ziva, and she suspected he didn't mind using it on strangers, too. He was probably unharmed, but he was wasting Pesah's very limited time with whatever he was doing. "I'll go find him."

Pesah nodded, and after a little hesitation at leaving Pesah alone, Ziva went. The little market teemed and hummed. People slipped around her, the crowd weaving itself around and past her. It smelled like a hundred different things: flowers and cooking meat and horse manure and cinnamon and sweat and earth. Ziva went from booth to booth, always watching for Almas but never seeing him.

Ziva paused by a booth festooned with a variety of fruits, arranged in such a way that they looked like a rainbow. The booth was crowded, and the woman serving the customers was rapidly trading money back and forth. A small child with her was helping customers select fruits from various piles.

Ziva's mouth watered as she beheld a pile of pomegranates. She didn't let herself stay and drool over the fruits. She forced herself to leave, and she walked past another fruit booth that had no customers at all. The two men at the booth watched the woman make all her sales with frowns on their faces.

On the other side of the market, in front of a booth filled with bread and pastries, Ziva found Almas. He was standing in front of the pastries, staring like he was entranced, and when Ziva said his name he didn't answer.

So she poked his arm. "Almas!"

He jumped. "What?"

"How long have you been staring at the pastries?" Ziva asked.

Almas rubbed his arm where she had poked him. "Not long. I like pastries, okay? How'd you sleep?"

"Fine," Ziva said. "Did you do any shopping at all?" He wasn't holding food, or anything, so Ziva knew the answer, but she wanted him to say it.

Almas said, "No. But I know where we are now. I know how to get to the city."

"Great," Ziva said. Almas was staring at the pastries again, so Ziva snapped her fingers in front of his face. "Come on, Almas. We need some food and then we'll go."

He nodded. "Okay. Um . . ." He lingered at the pastry table.

"Not pastries," Ziva said.

"What about bread?"

"Bread's good," Ziva said, and she stood by while Almas traded a few coins for a loaf of bread.

As they walked away, Ziva asked, "Where did you get the coins?"

Almas was quiet for a moment, then said, "Avag and Petros had a lot of money. And they weren't using it anymore. So . . ."

"So you stole it," Ziva finished for him, making sure her disapproval was obvious in her voice.

"They weren't using it!" Almas argued. "Plus, they owed me. They owed me a lot. More than I took."

Ziva couldn't argue with that. She still didn't know everything they'd put Almas through, and in the absence of that knowledge, she had to take his word. They approached the rainbow fruit table, and Ziva was about to suggest they buy some fruit to eat, when someone bellowed, "She shortchanged me!"

A man holding an apple in one hand pointed a big finger at the fruit vendor, who stood with wide eyes behind her money chest.

"Thief!" the man screamed.

The woman said, "Oh, I'm sorry sir. I didn't mean—"

"Everyone, count your money!" the man hollered. "She's stealing your hard-earned money!"

The patrons around the booth shifted uncomfortably. Some left, abandoning their fruit on the table. Others checked their money pouches.

Almas went to move past, but Ziva stopped. There was something about the man that was gnawing at her. Something about this whole situation wasn't right.

"Ziva, come on," Almas said.

But Ziva didn't follow.

The woman said, "I didn't mean to shortchange you, sir. How much did you give me?"

"An entire gold piece!" The man slammed the apple back down on the table. "I just want it back. I don't even want your produce. I'm going to spend my money with *ethical* vendors!"

Almas nudged Ziva with his elbow. "Let's go. This isn't our business."

Ziva ignored him. She watched the woman's face flash with anger for a moment, and then she opened the money chest. After a cursory glance, she said, "Sir, I don't have any gold pieces at all. Perhaps you thought you gave me gold, but it was bronze—"

"*Liar!*" the man yelled. "Thief!"

The woman's face was turning red, but she was trying to stay calm. "I don't have any gold pieces at all."

"You must have hidden it!" The man turned to the crowd. "Stealing your money! How many of you bothered to count your return coin carefully? How many of you did she rob?"

The woman said, "I haven't robbed anyone."

The man whirled, pointing at her child, who cowered behind her. "I bet that kid's been picking pockets!"

Now the woman looked outright angry, but the anger faded to fear when the crowd turned its attention to her child.

Ziva didn't look at the child. She looked at the produce booth nearby. One man stood behind it now, arms crossed, watching the exchange with a grin.

Almas said, "Ziva! Let's *go*."

But she couldn't.

Because she knew who this man was.

TWENTY-TWO

SHE LEFT ALMAS IN THE THROUGHWAY and charged up to the table, elbowing past customers until she was right next to the man claiming to have been robbed.

"Excuse me," Ziva said. But he didn't hear her.

He didn't notice Ziva's presence until she jammed one stiff finger into his belly while yelling, "Excuse me!"

Now he looked down and snapped, "What?"

She pointed to the produce booth across the way, which earlier had been staffed by two men, but now only one. "Isn't that your booth over there?"

The man's face reddened, and he bellowed, "Mind your own business!"

Ziva went through what Baba had told her about being a judge. Stay calm. Stay balanced. Don't let bias color the facts. She said calmly but loudly, "I passed by earlier and saw you standing behind that booth over there with that other man." She pointed. "But now he's all on his own. Why are you buying produce from another booth when you've got produce of your own?"

The man said, "Nonsense. That's not my booth."

"Why were you standing behind it earlier, then?" Ziva asked, arms crossed.

The crowd was looking between the man and the other produce booth now.

The man's red face was deepening to purple, and he said, "I didn't—"

"You know she didn't shortchange you," Ziva interrupted. "She doesn't have any gold pieces in that box. You gave her a different coin and now you're trying to make her look bad."

"I did so give her a gold piece!" the man said.

"I don't believe you," Ziva said, glaring up at him. "I don't believe you have any money at all. Your produce booth is failing because everyone buys from her and not you. I bet you stole that apple in the first place."

The man's furious scowl burned down at her as he opened his pouch and showed her a small collection of jingling bronze and silver coins. "I have plenty of money. I don't need to steal apples."

Ziva leaned forward to look into the pouch. The man's expression was jubilant, smug. Ziva turned to the woman, who was watching with wide eyes, and said, "How much does a single apple cost?"

The woman said, "Two bronze coins."

Ziva turned to the man. "You have enough bronze in there to buy several apples."

The man sighed. "What of it?"

"So why did you pay for a single apple with a gold coin?" Ziva asked. "If you had enough to just pay with bronze, why didn't you do that?"

The man hesitated, and someone in the crowd near him said, "That's a good question."

A woman in the crowd commented, "It's foolish to pay a gold piece for a single apple."

The man glowered down at Ziva, and she suddenly realized how small she was and how big he was. But she didn't move. She wouldn't back down. He was trying to ruin this woman's business to benefit his own. And that was wrong. Ziva couldn't stand by while he destroyed this woman's livelihood over a blatant lie.

The man hissed, "Listen here, you little brat . . ."

Trying hard to keep the fear out of her voice, Ziva pointed a little finger at him and said, "I've listened enough. Now *you* listen: you're doing a bad thing right now, and you need to stop. Leave this lady alone, and go sell your produce honestly."

Her finger was shaking, so she withdrew it. Her heart was beating so fast it rattled her ribs. But the palm tree brooch on her chest reminded her of Devorah, and her heart settled just a little bit.

The crowd quieted, watching, and then a man near Ziva put his hand on her shoulder and said, "She's right. I saw you at that other booth earlier."

The man blanched. "No. I was . . . uh, I was buying. I don't own it."

The crowd had changed. They regarded the man with frowns and scowls. He took a step away from Ziva, realizing that he'd lost the crowd. The people around him pushed forward, against him, shoving him away from the booth and away from the woman there who held her child against her. Ziva watched the man get ejected from the crowd. The other produce merchant remained at his table, watching what was happening with disbelief. The man who had tried to grift the apple lumbered toward the other booth, but at the last minute turned away and headed out of the market entirely.

Ziva breathed out long, shaky breaths. Baba would have been proud, she thought, and the thought of her father drove a spear of sadness into her heart. Baba was probably worried sick.

The man who had stood with Ziva patted her shoulder and said, "That was very brave. And observant."

"Thank you," Ziva said softly.

The man smiled and walked off, and Almas took his place.

"Ziva," Almas hissed. "That was incredible."

She shook her head. "I couldn't let that man lie like that. It could have ruined her business."

Almas said, "You care that much about someone you don't even know?"

Ziva didn't get the chance to answer before the child from the booth ran up. He held a small sack, and as he thrust it shyly at Ziva, he said, "Mama says thank you." As soon as Ziva took the sack, the child ran away again. She didn't even get the chance to thank him.

She looked in the sack. It was full of apples. Ziva looked up at the woman behind the table, who met her eyes and smiled. She couldn't look long, as she was still busy with customers, but she didn't have to. With warmth spreading in her chest, Ziva followed Almas back to the wagon, and she drove it out of the city while the three of them enjoyed the fruit and the bread.

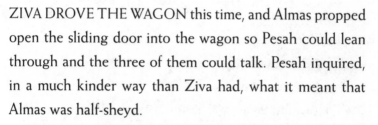

TWENTY-THREE

ZIVA DROVE THE WAGON this time, and Almas propped open the sliding door into the wagon so Pesah could lean through and the three of them could talk. Pesah inquired, in a much kinder way than Ziva had, what it meant that Almas was half-sheyd.

"Earlier I told Ziva that sheydim had three things in common with angels," Almas said. "But we've also got three things in common with mankind."

"Can I guess what they are?" Pesah asked, and Almas shrugged. "You can go in sunlight." He pointed to the apple in Almas's hand. "You eat food. And you, um . . . you grow old."

Almas laughed. "Close! Yes, we eat and drink like people do. And we get married and have children like people do. And we . . ." He hesitated, glancing at Pesah and then quickly away. "We die like people do."

Ziva glared at Almas, but Pesah breezed right past. "From old age?"

"That, and whatever else will kill a person."

Pesah's bandages shifted up in a grin. "So I was right about two things?"

Almas grinned back at him. "I guess you were."

"I should have guessed the having-children thing," Pesah said. "Since you're half-sheyd. That would make sense. But how does that work? I thought sheydim were invisible."

Almas pondered Pesah's question. "It's not about being invisible, I guess. It's about being able to not be noticed. Um . . . my mother could stand right next to someone and if she didn't want to be seen, they wouldn't see her. But she wouldn't be invisible."

"Oh!" Pesah said. "Can you do that?"

"No." He laughed. "I wish."

"That would be a good ability to have," Pesah said. "Are there a lot of half-sheydim?"

"I don't know. It's hard to tell." He indicated to himself.

Pesah squinted at Almas, like he was trying to discern any difference about him.

Ziva wasn't so sure. At the campsite, after she'd broken the bowl, Almas *had* looked different. But she couldn't explain how, so she didn't say anything. She just watched a raven marching about on the side of the road as they passed, poking its sharp beak into the grass for something.

"Sheydim eat," Ziva said. "Is that why you're obsessed with pastries?"

Pesah said, "Obsessed with what?"

"It's not like that," Almas said. "It's . . ." He looked bashful just then. "It might be stupid. But. Oh well. I've always wanted to bake pastries. Be the best baker in the land. I used to watch the bakers when I was little, turning flour and water into bread and tarts and treats, and it was like magic."

Ziva lifted an eyebrow. "You're a sheyd. You already have magic."

"Baking is edible magic," Almas said. "But that's not the kind of magic sheydim have. That's not what sheydim do."

Ziva narrowed her eyes at Almas. Of course baking wasn't the kind of magic sheydim did. Trickery was, and freezing people in place, and probably other nefarious things.

"You're only half a sheyd," Pesah said. "So maybe it can be what *you* do."

Almas's face warmed. He said softly, "Maybe."

Pesah said, "So your mother is a sheyd?"

Almas nodded as he chewed on a bite of apple flesh.

Pesah had his own apple, and he was trying his best to eat it without exposing his scarred face to Almas. "My mother isn't a sheyd, although Ziva might tell you otherwise."

Ziva turned her head to regard Pesah with a disapproving look, and then the raven from the side of the road landed on the bench between her and Almas, startling her into silence. It cocked its head at each of the children, who all stared at it with wide eyes, and then it bounced closer to Pesah and dropped something through the sliding door from its beak. Then it croaked and flew off.

The three of them were silent, staring, and then Almas said, "What just happened?"

Pesah had his head ducked down, then straightened up. In his bandaged fingers, he held a small pebble.

"It brought me a skipping stone," he said softly.

Ziva stared at the pebble with a tightening chest.

Almas said, "Why would it bring you a rock?"

"I don't know." Pesah held it out. "Do I keep it?"

Almas examined the pebble carefully. "I think so. It was a gift. You can't just throw that away."

Ziva said, "Birds don't give gifts."

"Well, that one just did," Almas said. He stroked his chin. "So curious."

"Can you hear a reason why the raven did that?" Ziva asked.

Almas scowled. "That's not how hearing the future works. This already happened. It's in the past now."

They were quiet for a while. The raven didn't come back, and finally Pesah said, "Hey, Almas. Tell us about the city we're going to."

Almas swiveled so he was facing Pesah. "What do you want to know?"

Pesah shrugged. "I dunno. The whole thing. Why can't the Angel of Death go there?"

Almas said, "In the time of the Garden of Eden, there were not only the normal animals that we know of now, but all manner of fantastical ones, too. And when Havva and Adam ate the fruit, they offered it to the animals. And all the animals ate the fruit, except one." He extended a finger up. "Just one. The Milcham bird." He threw his arms into the air. "An enormous bird with a man's face! He refused the apple, and for this reason was granted eternal life. And Hashem told the Angel of Death to build the Milcham a city to live in, called Luz, so he could be safe. When he finished, *malach ha-mavet* swore to the Milcham bird that he would never, ever set foot inside the city. For the Milcham's loyalty, he would never know the feeling of death, and the Milcham's feathers would even be capable of curing any ills. And when others discovered Luz was a refuge from death, they flocked there to hide, and live forever."

Pesah listened, enthralled. Ziva listened too, but didn't allow herself to fall into Almas's story as deeply as Pesah had. "So when we get there, we can just go inside?"

"Yep," Almas said.

"It's not guarded?" Ziva asked.

"Nope," Almas said.

If Ziva narrowed her eyes any further, they would be completely shut. Feathers that could cure all ills? Even leprosy? She tugged her sleeve over the pale spot on her wrist. "It doesn't make any sense that a city of immortality wouldn't be guarded at all."

Almas shrugged. "The story says anyone can go inside, except the Angel of Death."

To Ziva, that seemed too good to be true. There had to be some sort of downside to a city of eternal life, or else everyone in the whole world would be clamoring to get in. They rode for a while in silence, each digesting their separate thoughts about the city. A raven flew past the front of the wagon, dropping a cluster of small red berries onto the bench, and then flew off with a croak.

TWENTY-FOUR

BY THE TIME THEY STOPPED for the night, Pesah had a pile of varied gifts that had been brought to him by the ravens, who now perched freely on top of the wagon: coins, bits of fluff, sticks, and food. All manner of food. Some food had clearly been prepared by a person, and the raven stole it to bring to Pesah.

But mostly, the ravens brought skipping stones.

Pesah sat on a blanket that Ziva spread on the ground, examining his raven-borne treasure, while Ziva and Almas gathered wood and started a fire. They'd found a flat spot near a small pond, so the horses grazed on the plants around the pond and drank deeply of the water.

Ziva crouched next to Pesah and helped him go through his treasure. She held up a shiny rock and said, "Why do you think they're doing it?"

Pesah shrugged. "I guess they like me?"

Ziva smirked, then noticed Pesah staring at her wrist. The pale spot. She set the shiny rock down quickly, pulled her kaftan sleeve down, and stood up.

Pesah looked up at her. "Ziva . . . ?"

"My hands are so dirty," she mumbled, giving him a weak smile. "Road dust all over me. I better go, uh . . . wash my hands."

She hurried away from the fire that Almas was feeding with some bits of wood, down toward the pond. Maybe she could wash off this spot. It was just some whitish dust on her skin. It was fine.

She had already dipped her hands in the water when she heard Almas yell, "Ziva! No!"

But it was too late.

Something churned in the water, like it was boiling just in front of Ziva, and she stumbled backwards. A figure rose up out of the roil, with six wings spread wide and a seventh hanging limply to the side. She wore rags as clothing and no shoes, so Ziva could see her chicken feet plainly.

Ziva gaped up at her and said the only sheyd name she knew, other than Almas: "Shabriri."

"Oh my," the sheyd from the water said with a grin. "She knows my name."

Then Almas was there, grabbing Ziva by the arm. He pulled her away from the water, but Shabriri pointed a clawed finger at him and said, "You help the girl over your own kind?" She bared her teeth at him. "Betrayal."

"You're not harmed," Almas said. "Quit complaining."

Shabriri alit upon the pond's shore, the claws on her chicken feet leaving gouges in the wet dirt. She reached a hand toward Ziva and said, "You know the rules. She came close to the water." Shabriri lifted a hand to the sky. "And it's nighttime, isn't it? She must be punished."

Ziva refused to cower behind Almas, even though she really wanted to. The sheyd Shabriri wasn't like Almas. She was very tall, and shrouded in ethereal darkness that made the night deeper. Those chicken feet scratched idly at the ground, and Ziva took special notice of the spur on the back of each foot. Just like a rooster. Shabriri's one lame wing twitched.

"We both know it isn't about rules," Almas said. "You just like causing mischief."

Shabriri snorted. "Isn't that nice, hearing about mischief from one of the *kesilim*. What I do is artistry compared to your nonsense."

Kesilim. Fools? Why was she calling Almas a fool? From Almas's side, Ziva said, "You don't have to be rude."

Shabriri's terrifying gaze snapped to Ziva, who now did cower behind Almas. "Oh! Doesn't she know not to bring the attention of sheydim upon herself? No wonder you like this one, *kesil*. She must be so easy to manipulate."

Ziva's ears burned and she wanted to yell at Shabriri, but a question rose up for Almas instead. "What does she mean, manipulate?"

"Nothing," Almas said quickly. Too quickly.

Shabriri's laughter was like acid in the air, peeling layers of Ziva's skin away. "Oh dear, oh dear, little *kesil*! You've been found out, haven't you? Why don't you leave her to her punishment? Your work is done."

"I wasn't doing work!" Almas snapped.

"Of course not," Shabriri said, and winked at Almas.

Then, she turned her attention to Ziva again. "Don't worry, little girl." She lifted a clawed hand and stretched it toward Ziva. "You won't feel a thing."

The cold feeling that Almas had paralyzed her with was back, holding her in place. She couldn't look away from Shabriri's piercing eyes, and as she stared, everything started to go dark.

TWENTY-FIVE

NO. ZIVA COULD ONLY think it. Couldn't say anything. Almas's hands were on her shoulders but he couldn't move her.

Then Ziva heard Pesah yell, "Shabriri!"

Shabriri's smile fell away, and she looked up toward Pesah.

Then Pesah yelled, "Briri!"

Shabriri's scowl turned into an alarmed frown, and she muttered, "No."

"Riri!" Pesah yelled.

"No!" Shabriri roared. She let her hand drop, and Ziva's vision brightened again. The cold was gone. Whatever Shabriri had done was reversing itself.

"Ri!" Pesah yelled, and then he coughed hard. But whatever he had done was complete, and Shabriri walked backwards into the water until she was up to her chin. Her eyes glowed with malice and she smiled at Ziva.

"Saved by the boy with Death's mark upon his soul," Shabriri hissed. "Who will save you from yourself when he's dead?"

Ziva clenched her teeth and picked up a clod of dirt from the pond's edge. She hurled it at Shabriri, but the sheyd was gone, vanishing beneath the water with a final cruel cackle. The dirt hit the water harmlessly.

Ziva glared at the spot where Shabriri had disappeared for a moment, and then she rounded on Almas. Pesah was still coughing so hard he was retching. So she said nothing to Almas, just stormed past him and up to where Pesah was pitched forward, elbows on his knees, coughing wet and hard. He turned away from her and spit a glob of greenish stuff onto the ground.

"Ew," he croaked, coughing again. "Sorry."

She patted his back until his coughing fit subsided, and then she said, "Pesah. You banished a sheyd."

Pesah nodded and looked up at her with red eyes. "Yeah."

"Where did you learn that?"

"Synagogue," Pesah said. "When I used to go. The rabbi told us."

Ziva crossed her arms. "No one told the *girls* about it."

Pesah shrugged apologetically. "Well. Now you know."

Ziva glared at Almas as she asked Pesah, "Does it work on *all* sheydim, or just Shabriri?"

Almas blanched and said, "Ziva—"

"I *knew* we shouldn't trust you!" Ziva yelled. "You've been manipulating us!"

"No, I haven't!" Almas said.

Ziva stooped, picked up a small rock from the ground at her feet, and lifted her arm like she was going to throw it. "You'd better be honest with us right now, or I'm going to banish you, the way Pesah just banished Shabriri!"

Almas opened his mouth to say something, decided against it, and shut his mouth again. He was quiet, thinking, and then he said, "Okay. Um. Can I explain?"

"Honestly," Ziva said.

"Of course honestly," Almas said.

Ziva let her rock-throwing arm drop, but she kept the rock. "Explain."

Almas walked carefully up to the fire and stood on the other side. "Um. So. I told you my mother is a sheyd."

Ziva crossed her arms, and Pesah said in a wet voice, "Yes."

"Well." He rubbed the back of his neck. "She's one of the *kesilim*. Um . . . fooling spirits. In general they're mostly harmless, but they misguide humanity. Make them do stupid things."

Misguide.

Was that what Almas had been doing this whole time? Misguiding them? Running them in circles? Making them do stupid things?

Almas took a breath to continue, but Ziva held a hand up, silencing him. She trembled with fury. "Are you actually taking us to Luz?"

"Yes!" Almas said. "Where else would I be taking you?"

"I don't know!" Ziva said. "If you're misguiding us—"

"I'm not!" Almas said. "I'm not a full sheyd, so I can resist the temptation to do that. Plus, our deal supersedes any of my own desires. I *have* to help you get to Luz."

Ziva frowned. "Where's your mother? And your father, too. Why weren't they there when you were bound to that bowl?"

Almas's shoulders slowly slumped, and his defensive expression softened into sadness. "They, um . . ." His arms were limp at his sides. "They got sick. It was . . . the doctors called it *phthisis*. They coughed a lot." He pointedly looked away from Pesah. "And they stopped eating. They fevered all day and all night, and . . . then when they coughed, there was blood. I tried to get help, but no one would help me. The doctors didn't want to go near my parents because they were afraid they'd get sick themselves." He looked down at his hands, then let them drop. "But one of the physicians said he knew how to cure them, but I'd have to help. And I could help by telling him my real name. So I did. I didn't know the power in a name. I was too young, too scared. He bound me to that bowl, and he took me away from my parents, so I could serve him."

Ziva gasped, and Pesah murmured, "Oh no."

Almas shrugged, his face crumpling in on itself. "They probably died. They must have. I was the only one bringing them food or water or . . ." He hastily swiped his tears away. "It's okay. They're not suffering anymore."

Ziva's heart shrank in her chest, squeezing painfully. She couldn't imagine losing her parents. Or being taken forcibly from them. Or being tricked into servitude. Almas remained apart from them on the other side of the fire, and she wanted to call him over and comfort him.

But . . .

"Do you swear you're not misguiding us?" she asked.

Almas dried his face with his hands some more. "I don't know how to prove to you that I'm being honest, Ziva. I haven't done anything to betray either of you, but you still don't trust me."

Ziva hesitated, then said, "You're a sheyd, Almas."

"I'm *half* a sheyd," he snapped. "And what does that matter anyway—who my parents were, and what they did? You asked about my mother, but you never asked about my father. You assumed because he was a human, he was somehow better than her?"

Ziva bristled. "Your mother was a sheyd whose job it was to trick people! How can I know that and not be a little wary of you?"

Almas leveled a finger at her. "You don't get to talk about my mother anymore." His voice was low and dangerous, and Ziva saw his eyes flash.

From the ground Pesah held his arms up. "Hey, hey," he said. "Both of you. Ziva." He regarded her with his celestial eyes. "Would you like it if I judged you based upon Mama's actions?"

She frowned. She would not like that at all. "No."

"Even though you're her child?" Pesah said. "Of course you're just like her. Right?"

Ziva scowled now. "You know I'm not! She's vain and flippant, and she cares more about parties than her own son!"

An expression of shock lit up Pesah's eyes, and Ziva scoffed. "You thought I didn't notice how she never came to visit you?"

Pesah said softly, "She did, though. All the time."

"No, she didn't."

"She did," Pesah said. "She'd sit at the window and practice Greek with me. I mean, that's how she even knew to get me a cooking book as a gift."

The cooking book! Ziva had forgotten about it. "Sure, she got you a book in Greek. But it was a *cooking book*, Pesah. You don't care about cooking."

He was silent for a while. Almas watched, silent as well. The quiet dragged on and on, and then Pesah said, "Yes, I do."

His words were soft, but they smashed her into pieces. He cared about cooking? "Since when?"

"Since always," Pesah said. "But I got sick and I wasn't allowed in the kitchen. They didn't know if I would spread the disease in the food or something. So I couldn't go in the kitchen anymore, but Mama would bring me recipes and then make the ones I wanted. It wasn't the same as making them myself, but it was still nice."

Ziva just stared at him, her brain clicking, unable to process what he was saying. But then . . . the baklava on their birthday. The second Greek cooking book.

Pesah motioned to Almas. "His mother was a misguiding sheyd, and our mother . . . isn't perfect. She does care a lot about appearances and parties. And you don't. Not at all. If you're nothing like our mother, why does it mean Almas has to be something like his?"

She didn't know how to answer that, so she just stood there, silent.

Pesah turned to Almas. "Almas. My uncle Sabriel is a physician. If he came to you and offered help, would you trust him?"

Almas shifted on his feet. "No. Never."

"Even if I told you Sabriel is a good man?"

"No," Almas said.

Pesah put a hand on his own chest. "I want to be a doctor, too. Does that make me untrustworthy?"

Almas hesitated. "Well, you're not a physician."

Pesah nodded. "But I'm going to be one some day. And," he lifted a finger, "I already know how to banish sheydim. You've seen it. So what's stopping me from also knowing how to *bind* sheydim?"

Almas looked uncomfortable now. He took a step away from the fire, shrouding himself in darkness. "Nothing."

Pesah looked back at Ziva now. "Ziva, I trust Almas. He says he's taking us to Luz, and I believe what he says. And

Almas"—Pesah looked toward the sheyd, who was retreating into shadow—"I'm sorry someone you should've been able to trust turned out to be a monster. That's what that physician was. A monster. And if that means you don't trust me, then I understand. Once we get to Luz and your part of the deal is done, I won't hold it against you if you leave us forever. All I can do right now is swear that I'll never hurt you intentionally. And neither will Ziva." He looked up at Ziva now. "Right?"

She watched Almas standing mostly in shadow, and remembered how frightening he had been at the thieves' campsite, and the power he had to freeze her in place. He could have done that already if he'd wanted to. He could have left her frozen on the side of the road and left her to die. But he hadn't. He'd endured the same hardships of this journey that she had.

She absently put a hand on the brooch pinned to her kaftan. The brooch from her mother, who maybe hadn't just gotten it for her because it was pretty. Almas had brought it back to her, had specifically gone after Avag to retrieve it from him, because he'd gleaned that it was important to her.

And that was worth something, wasn't it?

Ziva swallowed hard; pride was bitter going down. "Right."

Almas said nothing. He lingered half in the flame for a moment, and then stepped backwards entirely into the darkness. Ziva heard his footsteps on the ground, walking away, and she let her shoulders droop.

"Pesah," she grumbled as she sank to her knees. "I'm such an idiot."

Pesah patted her on the back softly. "I know."

She snorted. "Thanks."

Pesah laughed. "Well, if it makes you feel any better, it's really easy to fix."

"How?"

Pesah nodded in the direction Almas had gone. "Go apologize to him."

Ziva felt herself bristling, but she knocked it down. "You're right."

"I know I'm right," he said, then coughed again. He spat more greenish mucus out of his mouth, pulling his bandages away so he didn't dirty them, and grumbled, "Hopefully in Luz they'll have something to stop the coughing."

"They will," Ziva said, and she sat with Pesah by the fire, waiting for Almas to come back. "I think I owe Mama an apology."

Pesah nodded. "You might."

"She bought me that Byzantine dress, though," Ziva said. "So I think she owes *me* an apology."

Pesah laughed softly. "That's true, too."

"When all this is over," Ziva said, "you and Almas can cook and bake together, and make big fancy feasts for the rest of us."

"When all this is over," Pesah agreed, but he sounded sad. "I'm tired, Ziva."

She helped him stand so they could make their way to the wagon, and she was alarmed by the heat coming off his skin.

It was just because they'd been so close to the fire, she told herself. That was it.

But she didn't really believe that.

TWENTY-SIX

ZIVA FOUND ALMAS SITTING DOWN by the water, throwing pebbles into it. She lingered a distance away until Almas said, "Pesah banished Shabriri. She won't come back until he's gone."

"I wasn't staying back because of Shabriri," Ziva said, even though that had been part of it. She wandered closer to Almas and sat an arm's length away from him. "I want to apologize."

Almas threw another few pebbles and then said, "So apologize."

"I'm sorry for—"

"Apology *not* accepted," Almas said.

"You didn't even let me finish!" Ziva said.

Almas said nothing. Tossed pebbles. Ignored her as she seethed in the darkness.

Ziva went through what Pesah had said to Almas and tried to figure out how she could say something similar. But she wasn't good at apologizing or admitting she was wrong. She had been really wrong about Almas. She'd judged him based on her own unfair bias. Baba said judges had to be fair above all else, or else the court of Atil might as well let mobs dictate justice. "If a man is brought to me accused of stealing," Baba had asked her once, "and he has stolen before, should I assume he is guilty because of his past, or allow him to prove that he has changed?" The latter, Ziva had said. The correct choice. Of course, that correct choice was easy to make while sitting in Baba's office without any risk attached to it. She sat in front of risk now, as he continued to throw tiny rocks into the water. Could she and Pesah afford to trust Almas?

She watched too many of his throws plunk in without a single skip, so she picked up a smooth rock and said, "You can't just throw them in. You have to angle and kind of . . ." She demonstrated, tossing the rock across the surface of the pond. It skipped along the dark surface, leaving perfectly round ripples in its wake.

Almas watched, then looked at Ziva. He lobbed a pebble at the pond without even trying to skip it, and it landed with a hollow splash and not a single skip.

Ziva sighed. "I made assumptions about you based on . . . nothing. And that was wrong. And I understand if you don't want to have anything to do with us after we get to Luz. So . . ." She hesitated, then stood. "I'll go. Just. Sorry."

She turned and took a couple steps, but stopped when he said, "You didn't make assumptions based on nothing."

Ziva turned. "Yes, I did. You've not actually done anything wrong."

Almas turned the current pebble he held over in his fingers. "You made your assumptions based on me being half-sheyd." He looked up at her. "If I were all human, would you be as suspicious of me?"

Ziva opened her mouth to say of course she would, and it wouldn't make a difference, and she would be mistrustful anyway.

But.

That wasn't true.

So she shut her mouth. And shook her head.

Almas nodded. "Even though you can't bind a human to help. There's no magic that'll do that. You'd trust a human—who can be just as evil, or even more evil, than any sheyd, by the way—over me, half a sheyd but bound by the laws of the universe to help you get to Luz." He tapped his chin and narrowed his eyes. "That doesn't seem to make sense, Ziva."

"I'm *sorry*—"

"I heard you the first time," Almas said, rolling his eyes.

"Well, I'll stop saying it, then," she said. "I can't fix how I acted before. I can just change how I act in the future. And if you still don't forgive me, or . . . not even forgiveness. I don't expect you to forgive me." She lifted her hands to the nighttime around them. "It's Elul. Um. It's the month before our New Year, and you're supposed to spend the month thinking about your actions over the past year, and—"

"Are you assuming right now that I don't know what Elul is?" Almas asked.

Ziva wanted to slap her own forehead. Yes. She had assumed. Of course a sheyd would know about Hashem and angels, but she had assumed he wouldn't be Jewish, that he wouldn't observe the holy days or celebrations or rites. "Yes," she mumbled.

"Huh," Almas said. He threw his pebble into the pond extra hard, angling it, and it skipped at least ten times before it sank under the surface.

Ziva groaned. "I'm just screwing this up the longer I stay here!"

"Then leave," Almas said. "Go to sleep." Then, with contempt dripping from his words, he added, "I'm not going to *do* anything."

"I know you won't," Ziva said. And she left him by the pond, curling up to go to sleep after she checked to make sure Pesah was still under his blanket.

In the morning, she got up before either of the boys and, after feeling Pesah's too-warm forehead and deciding not to wake him, washed in the pond. Then she sat on the bank where Almas had sat the night before, and she watched the sunrise turn the sky rosy.

She heard footsteps approaching from behind, and then Almas's voice: "Good morning."

Ziva glanced up at him as he stood by her. "Good morning."

They were quiet, and then Almas said, "I was angry last night. I'm sorry."

"You had the right to be angry," Ziva said. "I forgive you."

Almas watched the sunrise with Ziva. They were both silent, but it wasn't contentious.

Ziva said, "What are you going to do after you get us to Luz?"

Almas turned his head toward her. "What do you mean?"

"I mean, you'll be free of our deal," Ziva said. "So you can go do whatever you want."

"Yeah," Almas said. "I guess I can."

He sounded so sad when he said that, though.

"I wish you could go do what you wanted right now," Ziva said, assuming his sadness was because he'd gone from being bound to Avag and Petros, to being bound to Ziva and Pesah.

She smiled at him, but he didn't smile back.

"Who says I'm not already doing that?" Almas said.

Ziva said, "You want to travel across the world with us?" She absently put one hand over the pale spot on her wrist. "But what if you get sick? I mean . . . everyone said Pesah was going to make me sick. And he didn't. But. You know . . . what if?"

Almas poked his finger into the dirt a few times before answering.

"I couldn't save my parents," he said softly, focusing on his finger in the dirt. "Even if I hadn't been taken away, they would've died. I was really young. It wasn't my fault. But I still wonder sometimes, you know, what if someone had come along who could've helped them?" Now he looked up, meeting Ziva's eyes. "Maybe if I help you save Pesah, it'll . . . I don't know. I really needed someone and no one came, and then you two really needed someone, and I was there, so . . ." He shrugged.

Ziva sniffed and impatiently swiped a tear off her cheek. "Almas—"

"Plus," Almas said, cutting her off, "the first thing Pesah said to me was something kind. And I told you way back then that where I came from, kindness was enough."

"Good thing we were kind, then," Ziva said with a smile.

Almas blinked. "*We?* The first thing *you* said to me was something rude, and you tried to push me off a moving wagon!"

Ziva gasped at him. "You were trying to steal my wagon!" She laughed and shoved his shoulder. "I was kind eventually!"

He let her push him, joining her as she laughed. "Eventually!"

Ziva needed to wake Pesah so they could say their *selichot*, their penitent prayers that were special for Elul, and she let their laughter fade before asking, "Do you want to join Pesah and me to say prayers?" She added, "I know Pesah wouldn't mind. We would have invited you sooner, but . . ." She stuck her finger in the dirt and drew a squiggly line. "You know."

"I know," Almas said, but he was smiling. "I'd love to join."

They walked back up to the campsite. Ziva roused Pesah, who coughed for almost a full minute while she rubbed his back and Almas looked on with concern. Then the three of them prayed together, and Almas knew all the words, and when Ziva tried to apologize to him again for assuming he wasn't observant due to his sheyd-ness, he shook his head and said, "I forgive you, Ziva."

And that was that.

PART THREE

A kind demon, a sheyd of good character. Who would have imagined? Not me! And not Ziva either. But Almas had pledged to help the two of them, and he made good on his promise. And he prayed with them every day. He knew the landmarks: east and north, skirting past Atil and the crowds of Khazars returning to the city with their herds. Had Ziva's father and mother stopped looking for them yet?

East, still, beyond the borders of the khaganate and into the wild Blue Lands.

Further east. Into the steppe. Over rivers. Past mountains.

Ziva counted the days. One week. Then two. Rosh Hashanah drew nearer and nearer.

And all the while, ravens followed them, dropping rocks and treats into the wagon for Pesah. Pesah, who was growing more ill, who slept more often than he didn't, who barely ate the treats from the ravens.

When they had only three days remaining to Rosh Hashanah, Pesah could hardly open his eyes. His skin was hot where Ziva touched it, and his coughs were feeble.

Pesah was dying.

And then the wolves came.

TWENTY-SEVEN

ALMAS HAD FOUND A SMALL VILLAGE with an even smaller market, and Ziva waited with Pesah in the wagon as Almas used some of the coins the ravens had brought to buy some food. Pesah was flushed, breathing fast and shallow, skin slick with fever sweat. He didn't open his eyes when Ziva said his name.

With Almas gone and Pesah unconscious, Ziva could have cried. But she didn't. She couldn't. Because once she started crying, that was an admission, wasn't it? Of defeat, of knowing they weren't going to make it and Pesah was going to die. *Malach ha-mavet* would win.

She ground her teeth together.

No.

They had to make it to the city of eternal life. They *would*. They were close. They had to be. It had been almost a month since she had freed Almas. They had done so much work and come so far.

Almas was back with a small sack. He held it up. "Food, plus one of the vendors said I looked tired and gave me some tea to brew. It might help Pesah."

Ziva nodded. "We'll brew it when we stop to sleep tonight. Let's get going."

Almas hesitated. "How is he?"

"Sleeping," Ziva snapped. "We have to go, Almas. We have to get to the city."

Almas hesitated, then set the sack down. The hay pile was dwindling, but there was still enough of it to be a soft place for Pesah to lie on. Almas pointed to it and said, "Let him rest while we sit up front."

Ziva almost argued, but Almas's expression made her think again. He had that look on his face like he did sometimes, the look that meant he knew something that he just didn't want to say at the moment. So she nodded, made Pesah comfortable, and followed Almas to the front of the wagon.

Once they were on the road again, he handed her the sack of food. "I need you to help me watch for the final landmark."

"What's that?"

"An almond tree," Almas said. "Growing next to a cave. It won't actually be a cave. It will be a tunnel, and we'll go through it. The city is on the other side."

Ziva took a deep breath, blew it out, and said, "What does an almond tree look like?"

Almas described an almond tree, and it sounded to Ziva like any other tree. How was she supposed to tell it apart from a regular tree? As she looked around, she frowned. There weren't even any trees to be seen. They were on open steppe, with not a tree in sight. Even the distant mountains seemed treeless.

Ziva said, "We have three days, Almas."

He quirked an eyebrow at her. "Why do you say that?"

Ziva held her breath, wondering if she should tell Almas about Pesah's vision, and the Angel of Death coming on Rosh Hashanah. She decided not to, and instead said, "Um, my uncle Sabriel, the doctor . . . he says, when someone gets as sick as Pesah is now, they only have three days left."

"Huh," Almas said. "Well, I think we'll make it before then."

"I'm not so sure," Ziva said. She thought of how hot Pesah was, his burning skin and the sweat that clung to his temples. His fitful rest. His labored breathing. Her lower lip trembled and she stiffened it, keeping the tears inside. Crying meant defeat. And she refused to be defeated.

But it was getting harder to make that refusal.

They drove the wagon on, across the steppe, east. Ziva felt very small out here, in the engulfing fields that stretched long and low, under a sky that seemed so much bigger than it did in Atil. No clouds interrupted the striking blue of the heavens, and she asked Almas, "Is this why they call it the Blue Lands?"

He laughed. "I don't think so, but it fits, doesn't it? It's like the Red Lands, where I found you. The land itself isn't red. Just the direction from Atil."

"Why are directions told with color?" Ziva mused. It was something she'd known her whole life, but she'd never thought of why it was the way it was.

Almas shrugged. "It's always been that way. But I don't think it began at Atil, because the sea you would have to travel over to get to Constantinople is called the Black Sea. Black is north, right? And the Black Sea isn't north of Atil. It's north of Constantinople."

"So the Byzantines came up with color directions?"

"I don't think so," Almas said. "I think it's older than them."

"Is there a Red Sea as well?" Ziva asked. "And White and Blue Seas?"

Almas nodded. "You call the sea that Atil sits on *Bahr ul-Khazar*, the Khazar Sea. But its ancient name is the Blue Sea."

Ziva blinked at him. "It is not."

"Oh yes it is," Almas said, laughing. "What do you think people called it before the Khazars came?"

Ziva sat back on the bench. She hadn't ever thought about what the world was like before the Khazars. The Blue Sea, not the Khazar Sea. In the future, would it be called something different still?

"In the Blue Lands," Ziva murmured. "In Atil, we tell stories about the Celestial Khazars who stayed on the steppe out here. How they live the way we used to. They have no cities.

They just tend their herds." She watched the empty steppe before her, looking for any sign of the Celestial Khazars or their herds.

Nothing.

It was like she and Almas were the only ones there.

"They say other things, too," Ziva said.

Almas said, "Like what?"

"That the Celestial Khazars are shapeshifters," Ziva said. "They can turn into wolves."

In Atil, hearing stories of the wolves of the Asena . . . it was obviously a fairy tale. No one actually believed that they could turn into wolves. But out here in the Blue Lands themselves, Ziva wasn't so sure. The steppe radiated an intangible magic, like steam off cobblestones after a summer rain. Anyone living within that magic would certainly be magical themselves, so, why not turn into wolves?

She snorted derisively and looked at Almas for reassurance that no, in fact, people could not turn into wolves.

But Almas didn't look like he thought that was ridiculous.

He looked watchful.

TWENTY-EIGHT

THEY TRAVELED ALL DAY, but as dusk settled over the steppe, it didn't seem to Ziva like they'd made any progress at all. The mountains still seemed to sit on the horizon, and there had been no trees at all, almond or otherwise. No people. No animals except the ravens, still bringing scraps of food.

"I was hoping to find some water," Almas said. "But I don't want to go all night just to find some."

Ziva said, "There's water out on the steppe, isn't there?"

"Somewhere," Almas said, drawing the horses to a stop. "Just not anywhere we've gone."

They both sat on the bench for a moment, in their own thoughts. Ziva didn't know what Almas was thinking about. Her own thoughts were of Pesah, and how she was afraid to go into the wagon. Afraid to see if he'd gotten worse. What if he . . .

She didn't know if she could bear it if he died.

A realization hit her hard in the chest, knocking the breath out of her. She'd thought her mother had refused to visit Pesah. Refused to see him sick. Dying. Ziva had been wrong about that—apparently, her mother visited with Pesah all the time—but as she searched her memories, she realized Baba rarely visited. Ziva knew every step Baba's feet took, and they almost never took him to Pesah's house. Her heart ached, and anger began to flare there. How could he do that? Abandon Pesah? She'd noticed Baba's detachment, too, but hadn't really let herself think about it. He was supposed to be the one to do Pesah's amputations, but he wouldn't. So Ziva had to. He never talked about Pesah to anyone outside the family. He'd been the one to approve of sending Pesah away.

He's going to die anyway.

Baba treated Pesah like he was already dead.

Ziva's spark of anger kindled into a real fire, but it snuffed itself out fast.

She was afraid to go into the wagon and find that Pesah had died.

What if Baba was afraid of the same thing?

Her hands were shaking, so she balled them into fists. "I need to check on Pesah; then I'll help you start a fire."

Almas was looking out into the drawing darkness, and murmured, "I don't think we should start a fire tonight."

Ziva's skin prickled at the thought of spending the night in unbroken darkness. Even just a small fire was a reprieve from the night, keeping the nighttime creatures at bay. If they had no fire, what would drive away the demons that skulked in the shadows?

Then again, Almas was a demon. And he could skulk about perfectly fine in the daylight.

Before Ziva could tell Almas that she really wanted a fire, even just a small one, a howl broke the silence of the night. Long and lonely, forlorn, haunting. And very, very close.

Ziva grabbed Almas's arm and pulled herself closer to him. "Almas."

He said nothing. He picked up the reins. The horses had heard the howl, too, and were stamping their feet and swiveling their ears all around.

The howl faded, but before it was gone completely, another one answered it.

And another.

And another.

Almas smacked the reins on the horses' flanks and yelled, "Hyah!"

The horses ran. It was barely light enough to see where they were going. Ziva gripped the bench and prayed they wouldn't hit a ditch, which would break a horse's leg or a wagon axle.

The howls followed.

Movement to Ziva's side caught her attention, and she swiveled her head to look. A gray wolf was running alongside the wagon. She had never seen a real wolf before, but she had always imagined them to be the size of a large dog. But she had been wrong, because this one was almost as big as the horses. Its eyes glowed yellow in the dimness, and as she watched, a second wolf came abreast of the first one. They kept pace with one another for a moment, and then the second one put on speed and ran ahead. It ran beside the horses now, huge and silent, its fanged mouth open.

"*No!*" Ziva bellowed, the sound starting in her belly and thundering up.

The wolf startled and glanced back at her, looking confused—if wolves could look confused. Then it went back to focusing on the horse, and Ziva grabbed the bag of food on the bench. She reached in, snatching the first thing that her fingers touched, and she hurled it—a fig—at the wolf's head.

The fig hit the wolf and bounced away harmlessly, but it still made the wolf look back at her again. Ziva grabbed another thing out of the bag, an apple that time, and she was about to throw it when Almas said, "Ziva, don't!"

She snarled, "It's going to kill the horses!"

"No it isn't!" Almas said. "Look."

She did. He was pointing on his side of the wagon, where two wolves mirrored what the wolves on Ziva's side were doing. The two that flanked the horses didn't jump to attack. They occasionally swerved slightly to one side or the other, and the horses turned with them.

"Almas," Ziva gasped. "They're leading the horses somewhere."

Almas still held the reins, but he didn't try to steer the horses. He glanced down at the wolf running near him on his side, and the animal looked up at him. And woofed.

He said, "Ziva. Do your stories of the Asena say whether they're nice or not?"

Ziva said, "No. Just that they didn't want to move into the city. Why?"

Almas pointed ahead. "Because I think we're about to meet them."

Silhouetted in the darkness was a mass of something, and as they drew closer, Ziva realized it was a camp of wagons all pulled around in a circle. People formed a crowd before the camp. Some were on foot, but most were mounted. Within the crowd were several giant wolves, standing still. Watching.

The wolves leading the horses slowed, and the horses slowed with them. Ziva slid closer to Almas, dredging up any story she'd ever heard of the Asena, hoping there wasn't some blood feud she was unfamiliar with, hoping that they wouldn't hold her hostage. Hoping, mostly, that maybe they knew the way to Luz.

The wagon came to a stop just in front of the Asena standing in front of their wagons. Up close, Ziva noticed their bows, their knives, their swords. She swallowed hard.

An old woman came forward. She leaned on a walking stick and stopped just before Ziva's horses. She patted each one on the snout, and then looked up at Ziva with eyes as blue as the land around them.

"Who are you?" the old woman asked. "And why have you brought Death here?"

TWENTY-NINE

ALMAS AND ZIVA TRADED a terrified glance, and Ziva thought of the Angel of Death. Its shadow, full of eyes, burning, pointing at Pesah.

"Pesah," she breathed out, and she threw open the sliding door. Inside, Pesah was sleeping fitfully. His breaths were ragged in his chest. Ziva touched his forehead, tears pricking her eyes as the heat coming off him seeped into her own fingers. He was flushed, cheeks red and splotchy and damp.

Ziva held him, biting her lip hard to keep from crying. The back door of the wagon opened, and Almas stood there with the old woman. The woman handed Almas her stick and then climbed into the wagon, grunting the whole time. She trundled over to Ziva, squatted on the other side of Pesah, and said, "Ah. Here is why Death follows."

"We came here to save him," Ziva said. Her voice trembled.

"Did you?" The old woman stroked her chin. Then she touched Pesah's forehead, right in the middle, with a single finger. "He will die in one day."

"Three days," Ziva said, and the old woman looked surprised. "He saw a vision. He'll die on Rosh Hashanah, in three days." She went through the days in her head, making sure she hadn't missed some. But no. It was still three days to Rosh Hashanah. Had his vision been wrong? Had it changed?

"A vision, hm?" The old woman stroked Pesah's bandaged forehead gently. "Sometimes visions are wrong."

"Not this one," Ziva said, hating the desperation in her voice. "Please. I . . . I brought him here to save him. To find the city of Luz."

The old woman blinked long and hard at Ziva. Her face was etched with the wrinkles of a long life in the sun. She didn't look like the other Khazars of Atil. Her face was perfectly round, her hair perfectly black in a long braid that hung over her shoulder. Her hooded, deep-set eyes were as blue as Pesah's, sparkling even in the dimness of the wagon. She wore a kaftan—like a proper Khazar—that was embroidered with intricate scenes of horses and wolves and birds. The birds looked like ravens to Ziva.

She set her soft, wrinkled hand on Ziva's and said, "My name is Chichäk. Where have you come from?"

"I'm Ziva," she said. "We came from Atil." She motioned vaguely in the direction she believed to be west.

Chichäk rocked back on her heels. "A city tribe! But where have you *come from?*"

For a moment, Ziva didn't know what Chichäk was asking. She'd told her where she came from. Atil. Maybe she wanted to know their journey exactly.

But then she realized. "I'm a Red Khazar." She pointed to Pesah. "*We* are Red Khazars."

Chichäk nodded thoughtfully. "I guessed, I guessed." She fingered Ziva's brow band, which had been a brilliant red three weeks ago, but now was starting to just be dirty. "Red. The color of blood. Of fire." She grinned at Ziva. "You carry the redness deep within you. But red also means anger. Quick to react." Now she regarded Ziva not with a grin but with a knowing stare. "Quick to judge."

The urge to say that she was *not* quick to judge rose in Ziva, but she swallowed it down.

Chichäk patted Pesah. "I think I can help you."

Ziva breathed out hard, relief washing over her. "You know where the city is?"

Chichäk said, "No. Maybe someone else here does. But I can help with him." She nodded at Pesah. "He's too ill to travel. He will die tomorrow if you go on with him like this. I can ask for him to be healed."

Ziva said, "Ask who?"

Chichäk smiled. "Whoever will listen."

THIRTY

MOST OF THE STRUCTURES in the Asena camp were wagons that had been arranged in a circle. But outside that circle was a single stationary building, set a little apart from all the wagons. Chichäk called four young men to carry Pesah over to that building, but when Ziva tried to go inside, Chichäk stopped her.

"I need to be alone with him," Chichäk said.

"Why?" Ziva demanded.

Chichäk held Ziva's hands in hers. "I will ask a great many spirits for help tonight. I don't want them to become confused about who I need help with."

Ziva didn't understand what Chichäk was saying, but she didn't have time to ask for clarification before the old woman squeezed Ziva's hands and vanished into the tent.

"Wait!" Ziva tried to follow her in, but the four young men who had carried Pesah blocked her way, shaking their heads apologetically.

"Go back to the circle," one of the young men suggested. "You can put your horses up and have dinner."

"I'm not hungry," Ziva said, even though she was.

A raven alit upon the little building, just over the entrance, and the four guards watched it perch.

"You're lucky," one of them said to Ziva. "A spirit has decided to come."

Ziva dismissed the raven's presence with a wave of her hand. "That's just a raven. Those birds have been following us for weeks."

The young man blanched. "For weeks?"

"Yeah." Ziva crossed her arms. "Bringing my brother treats and stuff. Filling our wagon with junk."

The four young men stared at her, gaping. One said, "You should go put your horses up," and then they all ignored her.

The raven croaked on top of the building, cocking its head to turn one shiny eye at Ziva. She looked at it just in time for it to leap off the building and fly away, toward the east. Chichäk's four guards didn't look like they were about to leave the entrance unguarded, so Ziva stalked away. She went to find her wagon, and when she did, saw Almas putting the horses up. She stopped before she got close enough for him to notice her, shrouded in darkness, realizing she didn't want to sit with anyone or talk to anyone just then. She was frustrated and annoyed and . . . afraid. And she didn't want Almas to see her like that.

So she turned around and sat outside the wagon circle, just outside of the reach of light from the bonfire in the center. The Asena gathered around the fire, eating and laughing. An old man told a story to some children, and the children squealed with delight a couple of times. There were no wolves to be seen. Only people.

Ziva stared into the dancing shadows thrown by the fire, and thought of Pesah. Would Chichäk be able to help? She snorted. *Spirits*. Chichäk was asking for spirits to help Pesah, and there was no such thing as spirits. This was a waste of time, and if Chichäk was right, Pesah didn't have time to waste.

She wasn't right, though. Pesah had seen a vision. Rosh Hashanah. They had until Rosh Hashanah.

The shadows dancing off the fire changed. Ziva was back at Avag and Petros's camp, and they were screaming, and the shadow with wings and burning eyes was there, stretching across the ground.

Ziva blinked, banishing Avag and Petros, but the winged shadow remained.

Her breath snagged in her throat, a scream strangling there, and she startled back. Looked up. And saw . . .

A boy.

The winged shadow was gone. A little boy was walking carefully to her.

Ziva put her hand to her own forehead. Was she fevering now? Hallucinating?

The boy looked to be eight years old, maybe nine. He had the same round face as Chichäk, but his hair wasn't as black as hers. His kaftan was a simple gray with wooden button closures, and he stopped a few feet away from her and said, "Would you like some baklava?"

Ziva's mouth watered immediately. It had been weeks since she'd even seen baklava, let alone tasted some. "You have baklava here?"

The little boy held out both hands. In each palm, he held a single square of the treat. "Of course."

She desperately wanted that baklava, but she forced herself to shake her head. "I don't want to take your sweets from you. But thank you."

The little boy approached fully, sat down in front of her, and extended a hand. "I'll have one, and you have one."

Ziva almost reached for it, but her stomach felt sour. So she shook her head again and said, "Thank you. Really. But I don't feel very good." She offered him an apologetic smile. "Maybe tomorrow."

He nodded, withdrew his hand, and said, "Why are you all alone?"

Ziva sighed. She pointed to the building where Chichäk was with Pesah. "My brother is sick."

"Are you sad?"

"Yes," Ziva said. And angry. But she didn't add that part.

The boy took a bite of baklava, chewed a few times, and then said, "He's going to die soon."

Whatever smile Ziva had been able to manage on her face fell off, dropping hard to the ground like a bird shot from the sky.

The little boy saw her face change and pointed to the bonfire. "I heard someone say so."

Ziva managed to say, "Well, they don't know anything."

"Chichäk is a good shaman," the boy said. "But he's very sick."

"I'm going to save him," Ziva said. "There's a city out here in the Blue Lands. It's called Luz. And inside it, there is no death. I'm taking him there."

The boy watched her talk, taking another bite of his baklava. And then he said, "I know how to get to Luz."

THIRTY-ONE

ZIVA'S HEART JUMPED, BUT THEN crashed back down. A child? How did a little boy know where Luz was? "Will you tell me how to get there?"

"Sure," the boy said. "But first you have to talk to me."

"About what?"

The boy shrugged. "Out here, there is no fear of Death. It comes when it comes. Sometimes you can bargain, and the spirits will help you. Sometimes they can't help, and Death comes anyway." He regarded her with eyes the color of moss. "Why do you fear Death?"

Ziva frowned at him. "I don't."

"You ran all the way from Atil to get away from it."

She opened her mouth to ask him how he knew that, but then remembered she had told Chichäk she was from Atil. Word had spread fast within the wagon circle.

"I wasn't running to get away from Death," Ziva said, even though she sort of had, hadn't she? "Everyone kept telling Pesah he was going to die. They wouldn't even try to help him. And . . ." She took a deep breath. "And I'm not going to sit by and just let him die."

"So you're not running from Death," the boy said. "You're fighting it?"

Ziva said, "Not fighting. I don't know. Resisting. Challenging."

The boy smiled. "That's what Chichäk is doing with the spirits. Asking them to challenge Death for your brother."

Ziva snorted. Spirits. It was nonsense.

"You don't believe in spirits?" the boy asked. He didn't look or sound upset, but Ziva felt bad anyway for snorting at his beliefs.

She said, "Sorry. I shouldn't have laughed."

"It's okay," the boy said. "You're the city faith. The other Khazars left behind the old ways. Mostly."

Ziva couldn't imagine any of her forebears believing in spirits. Her grandfather, Benyamin, had been very strict when it came to observance of Jewish custom. He never would have let Pesah be looked after by a shaman. If Ziva's grandmother had known that she had just spent nearly a month sleeping in the same wagon as a boy she wasn't related to—one that was half a sheyd, even!—Nene Khatun would probably have fainted from shock.

The boy continued: "The Blue Khazars follow Tengri. Do you know Tengri?"

"No," Ziva said.

The boy pointed upward into the darkness. "Tengri is the god of the sky."

Ziva smiled at him, trying to keep it from looking as patronizing as it felt. "In the city, we believe in Hashem."

The boy said, "Do you think they're different?"

"Of course they're different," Ziva said.

"Are they?" The boy cocked his head to the side. He held up his hand. "Mankind has been given five fingers, because one finger would not be enough."

Ziva stared at the boy, whose splayed hand was sticky with honey and baklava crumbs. "So?"

"So," the boy said. "There are many paths to the heavens. Because one path would not be enough."

Ziva looked away from him, into the darkness. This boy was saying Hashem and their god, Tengri, were the same thing? Would that mean the god of the Byzantines, and the god of the Arabs, and the god of the Persians, and the many gods of the Geats—they were all the same, too?

"We don't believe in spirits, though," Ziva said.

The boy nodded, letting his hand drop. "Who is Death, to you?"

"An angel," Ziva said.

"Can you see this angel?"

Ziva thought of the shadow on the ground. "Sometimes. A little. But not really."

"Are there things other than angels?"

"Yes," Ziva said. "Demons. Sheydim. We can see them, too."

"What do the angels and the demons do?" the boy asked, eyes wide, looking absolutely enthralled by the conversation.

"Angels are good," Ziva said. "And demons are . . ." She thought of Almas and his mother. "Demons are complicated."

"Angels are good?"

"Yes."

"Even the Angel of Death?"

Ziva opened her mouth to say no, the Angel of Death was *not* good, but then she shut her mouth again. Death was an angel. And angels were good. They did the work of Hashem. The Angel of Death did the work of Hashem. By killing.

"Death is good sometimes," Ziva said slowly. "I guess. But not for Pesah."

"Why not for Pesah?" the boy asked.

"Because he's special."

"Special how?"

Ziva let out a slow breath. "He's smart. He's *so* smart. He's brilliant."

"And brilliant people can't die?"

"Yes, they can," Ziva said. "But losing brilliant people . . . Pesah's disease takes the lives of a lot of people. Pesah's smart enough to find a cure for it. So, if he dies, it means more people will die, because he won't be around to make the cure."

The boy blinked. "Pesah is the only person ever who can find a cure?"

"No," Ziva said, struggling to find a better argument. "I'm sure someone else could. But—"

"So Pesah *can* die?"

"No!" Ziva snapped. "He can't die. He can't. Because . . ."

She stared into the darkness. Pesah couldn't die, because then Ziva would be alone. She would miss him too much. She didn't know if she could stay on her feet without Pesah there.

The two of them sat in silence for a while, and then the boy stood up. "I have to go."

"Okay," Ziva said softly. "Good night."

The boy lingered. He pointed into the distance. "Do you remember the mountains over there?"

She'd watched them all day, hoping they would get closer, and they never had. She nodded.

"*The city of eternal life,*" the boy said softly, almost chanting. "*Take the blue road to its end, then black until the sun is gone. The bitter flower, the cavern dark, then red, then red, then red.*"

Ziva watched him, her stomach twisting. The way he spoke . . . the cadence of his words. Soft lilting, up and down and down. Like being in synagogue.

He trailed off, staring into the distance, and then laughed. "That's what the songs say!"

Ziva said, "Thank you for sharing it."

Where he stood, the boy was backlit by the bonfire from the camp; he seemed to glow. "But once you're there, you can never leave. Death waits outside the city, and anyone who steps outside . . ." He snapped his fingers.

Then the boy turned and ran off into the darkness, and soon Ziva was alone again, with only a few crumbs of baklava in the dirt as proof the boy had ever been there.

THIRTY-TWO

ZIVA DREAMED ABOUT the Angel of Death, who was standing at the threshold of some room Ziva was hiding Pesah in. The *malach* said nothing, just knocked steadily on the door, and Ziva held Pesah tight. Then the *malach* was there, inside the room, grabbing Ziva's shoulder, and in her dream, she screamed.

Someone was grabbing her still, shaking her softly, and she startled awake with a scream half-formed in her throat.

Almas knelt over her, withdrawing his hand with wide eyes. "Ziva?"

She got her bearings. She was in the same spot she'd been when the little boy with the baklava had come the night before, curled up on her side in the grass and dirt. She felt stiff and cold from the night out in the open, even though at some point someone had draped a blanket over her.

Almas watched her look around with sleepy eyes. "Are you okay?"

Ziva nodded. "I was dreaming," she said. She didn't tell him about what.

Almas said, "That old woman, Chichäk, wants to talk to you."

Her heart tripped. Chichäk was going to tell Ziva something about Pesah. He was either better, or unchanged, or . . .

No. It wasn't Rosh Hashanah yet. He had until Rosh Hashanah.

Almas pulled Ziva off the ground, and the two of them went to Chichäk's little building. Two of the four young men from the night before were still there, and Chichäk stood with them. She looked very tired, but pleased.

As Ziva approached, Chichäk reached out her arms and grinned. "The spirits have answered!"

Ziva didn't dare hope that Pesah was cured. She just hoped he was well enough to travel. "How did they answer?"

Chichäk motioned to the door of the little building, and as she did, the flap was pushed aside. The two other guards emerged, flanking a Pesah who looked absolutely exhausted, but awake. Not fevering. He was breathing hard, but he was up.

When he saw Ziva, he brightened. "Ziva!"

"Pesah." The word fell out of Ziva's mouth and she ran to him, looping her arms under his and hugging him as tightly as she dared. His bandages had been changed and he smelled herb-y, as if Chichäk had applied some sort of salve under them.

Chichäk watched from beside Almas. "He's been granted a reprieve only, I'm sad to say. The spirit of Death was very clear about that. Long enough to arrive at the city"—she motioned vaguely toward the mountains in the distance—"but not beyond."

"That's all we need," Ziva said to her, then looked at Pesah. "Two days. We can get there in two days."

Pesah nodded, and the two guards helped him to the wagon, which had been cleaned up, and restocked with hay and food and other supplies sometime during the night. The two horses weren't harnessed to the cart, but rather were trotting around with the Asena horses. They had both been groomed, tails braided with colorful red and blue yarn twined within.

The entire Asena tribe was there to see them off, it seemed. Ziva didn't have to do anything at all, just stood by Pesah as people arrived to hitch the horses to the wagon, to help Pesah into the back, to double-check wagon wheels and axles, to strap all their new supplies down in the back so nothing rolled around. Almas climbed onto the bench, taking up the horses' reins.

Chichäk stood by, smiling at Ziva, and before Ziva could think herself out of it, she hugged the shaman. Chichäk hugged her back with arms that felt as big as the whole world, as warm as a sunny afternoon, and as sweet as baklava.

"You're a very brave girl," Chichäk whispered to Ziva. "I hope you find what you're looking for."

"I will," Ziva said. "Thank you for all you did for Pesah."

Chichäk released Ziva from her hug and patted her on the cheek with a motherly smile. "Be safe."

Ziva nodded and climbed on the bench beside Almas. He clicked his tongue, and the horses pulled the wagon forward, toward the mountains. Ziva stared at the distant snow-dusted tops, knowing Luz was past them somewhere.

They cleared the Asena wagon circle, and then Ziva spotted the little boy standing off to the side. Almas drove the wagon past, and the little boy raised a hand at Ziva. Ziva waved back, and then the wagon was past him, and when she turned to find him again, he was gone.

THIRTY-THREE

ZIVA SLID THE DOOR OPEN so she and Almas could talk to Pesah while he sat inside the wagon.

The first thing Pesah said was, "They gave us so much stuff, Ziva!"

"Good," Ziva said. "Better to have too much than too little."

"I guess," he said.

Almas swiveled to look at Pesah. "What was it like?"

Pesah looked up at him, confused. "What was what like?"

"You nearly died!" Almas said, and Ziva smacked him on the arm with the back of her hand.

"Almas," she scolded.

"Sorry," he said. "But I've never met someone who nearly died and then came back. I want to know what it was like."

Ziva scowled. "I don't think Pesah wants to talk about that."

"No, I don't mind," Pesah said. He looked down at his bandaged hands. "It was . . . I don't remember much. I remember being in the wagon on and off, and then someone carried me into that tent, and then a raven came and spoke to me."

Ziva tensed. There *had* been a real raven. It had landed on top of the building and then flown off. But it was just one of the ravens that insisted on bringing Pesah treats. She was sure of it.

Right?

Almas was enthralled. "What did the raven say?"

"It said, 'take the blue road, take the blue road,'" Pesah said, squawking the words out. "And I asked why, and the raven told me it would be right back, and it flew away."

"The blue road," Almas mused. "What's that mean?"

Ziva and Pesah glanced at one another. They had never told Almas about Pesah's vision. Ziva lifted her eyebrows at Pesah, and after a moment, Pesah nodded.

He said, "Almas, we didn't tell you something about . . . about me, and why we left, and all that."

Almas said, "What do you mean?"

Pesah sighed, then coughed. Still wet. Still deep in his chest. "I had a vision. Um . . . at our birthday party." He pointed to Ziva. "And I had a terrible headache, and then I had a vision of myself standing on a blue road in a red land on Rosh Hashanah."

Almas stared, mouth hanging open a little, and said nothing.

Pesah continued. "Someone stood on the road with me. It was a man, and . . ." He paused for a long time. "I think I told Ziva that he had too many eyes. Right?"

Ziva nodded. "And while you had the vision, you said *malach ha-mavet.*"

"Oh yeah," Pesah said. "I forgot I said that."

Almas blurted, "You saw a vision of something with too many eyes *and you said* malach ha-mavet *out loud?*"

Pesah nodded, and Almas let his head drop forward. He rubbed his eyes as he said, "So when you saw *malach ha-mavet* at the camp, that wasn't the first time?"

"I didn't see anything at the camp," Pesah said.

Almas pointed to Ziva. "She did."

"It doesn't matter," Ziva said, annoyed. "A blue road in a red land from your vision, and then you say that raven told you to follow the blue road?"

Pesah nodded. "I don't know what that means, though. These are the Blue Lands, not red ones. Red would be . . ." He motioned off to the south.

Almas said, "A blue road in a red land sounds like we would be in the south, on a road going east. But we're east, and still going east." He rubbed his chin. "A blue road in a blue land."

Ziva said, "Well, on the blue road in the red land, Pesah meets the Angel of Death. So we don't want to be in the red land." She pointed to the mountains. "Those are east of us. We're on a blue road. And the Asena boy told me that Luz was past the mountains."

Pesah startled and grabbed Ziva's hand. "What Asena boy?"

"I don't know." Ziva shrugged. "I didn't learn his name. While I was waiting for you last night, he came and sat with me and we talked. He said he knew how to get to Luz."

Pesah stared at her. She couldn't figure out what the look in his eyes was, or why it unsettled her so much.

"What?" she asked.

He blinked and looked away from her. "Nothing."

Before Ziva could press Pesah for more, Almas said, "Speaking of directions to Luz—Ziva, what are they, exactly?"

She watched Pesah for a breath more, and then looked up at Almas. "Um, go east until we get to the mountains. Then turn north, he said." She pointed to the left, toward the northern end of the mountains. "Then follow the road north until sunset, and then we'll see a flowering almond in front of a cave."

Almas said, "I told you we had to find an almond, didn't I?"

"Yes, you did."

"And a cave."

"Yeah, you were right," Ziva said. "I never said you were wrong."

"Who told you about this?"

"The little boy," Ziva said.

"How did he know about it?" Almas asked.

Ziva shrugged. "I don't know."

Thoughtfully, Almas watched the horses walk for a little while, and then he said, "Maybe that boy is half-sheyd, too."

THIRTY-FOUR

THEY REACHED THE FEET of the mountain at midday and rested under the canopy of the forest that was thin but there. As Ziva dug through all the food the Asena had gifted them, she heard a croak from behind her. When she looked, a raven was perched in one of the trees, watching her.

She turned and put her hands on her hips. "I thought you and your friends abandoned us."

The raven cocked its head.

"Feh," Ziva said, and went back to the food.

Almas helped Pesah get out of the wagon so he could sit in the grass. Ziva brought some flatbreads and dried meat, handing some to her brother and some to Almas. As she did, Almas said, "If we won't reach the almond tree and the tunnel until sunset, should we wait before we go inside? Stay the night outside the tunnel, and then travel through it in the morning when there's light?"

"No," Ziva said. "We need to get there as fast as possible."

Almas chewed thoughtfully on his bread until Ziva sat down with hers. "Well, as long as we get there before Rosh Hashanah, we're fine, right?"

"Yeah," Ziva said, "but I'd still rather not risk it."

"Did that Asena boy tell you how far beyond the cave the city was?" Pesah asked. "Once we get through the tunnel, I mean. Is it right there?"

"I don't know," Ziva said. She turned to Almas. "Do you know?"

He shook his head. "I just know that it's somewhere."

They ate in silence, each caught up in their separate thoughts. Pesah was the first to speak, asking Almas, "What is Luz like?"

Almas shrugged. "A city of immortality," he said. "Where no one dies. No one is sick."

Pesah asked, "Will I be able to read? And make medicines? Does anyone ever come there with news from the outside?"

"I don't see why not," Almas said.

"Will I still grow old?" Pesah asked. He held up one diminished hand. "Will the city heal me?"

Almas said, "I don't know."

Pesah let his hand drop and stared into the distance, thinking.

Ziva said, "Maybe it will heal you. But even if it doesn't, at least you won't lose any more fingers."

Pesah nodded. "And I bet, since no one can get sick, they won't mind me being around. I'll be able to mingle with people."

"You could go to parties again!" Ziva said, laughing.

A raven chose that moment to land in front of Pesah and drop a pebble on the ground in front of him. It flew off, and Pesah picked up the pebble.

Almas leaned over to get a closer look at the little stone. "Pesah, did you ever . . . rescue a baby raven or something?"

"I don't think so."

Almas scratched his head. "I don't get it, then. Why have they been following us this whole time? Bringing you treats?"

Pesah shrugged, and Ziva thought of the raven that had perched on top of Chichäk's healing hut, and what one of the guards had said: *A spirit has decided to come.* She snorted. Spirits.

But . . .

She searched the trees for the raven, and didn't see it anywhere.

"Almas," Ziva said, "are there any sheydim who can turn into ravens?"

Almas stroked his chin. "I don't know. I don't think so."

"Or *malachim?*"

"Why would a *malach* turn into a raven?" Pesah asked.

Ziva plucked at grass. "I don't know. I saw a raven at the Asena camp and they said it was a spirit. I thought, well, spirits aren't real. But maybe it was a *malach*, being watchful." She shrugged. "And Pesah dreamed of a raven. Didn't that dream-raven say it would be right back, Pesah?"

He nodded, rolling the pebble between his fingers. "Do you think this is what it meant?"

"Maybe."

They were silent again. A gentle breeze rustled Ziva's hair.

"So, Almas," Pesah said. "When you can get to an oven and bake something, what's it going to be?"

Almas blew air up, so it rustled the hair falling over his forehead. "I don't know. What should I make?"

They were all thoughtfully quiet, then Ziva said, "Challah." She missed the fresh loaves of challah every Erev Shabbat.

Almas nodded. "Challah would be good. What about you, Pesah?"

"Baklava," Pesah said.

"Ooooh," Almas said. "I love baklava."

Ziva said, "The little boy at the Asena camp had baklava."

Pesah sighed. "Lucky. I'd love some right now. Ever since I woke up at the Asena camp, I felt like . . . I dunno, like I'd been eating it in my sleep. I could taste the honey."

Almas looked pensive, forehead creased in thought. "The little boy who told you about Luz is the same one that had the baklava?"

Ziva nodded. "Yep."

"Huh," Almas said thoughtfully. "I wonder where he got it. I didn't see anyone else with some."

"He had a hidden stash, maybe," Ziva said. "He offered me some, but I didn't take any."

Pesah sighed again. "I wish you had, so you could have given some to me."

Ziva laughed, but Almas didn't. He said, "No. I think it's better that you didn't take it." And he didn't say anything else until they were on their way north.

THIRTY-FIVE

THE RAVEN FOLLOWED THEM NORTH, hopping from tree to tree at first but then settling on the top of the wagon like an ornament. Pesah held out some food to it, but it didn't take any.

Almas drove the wagon silently, wrapped up in thought. Ziva sat against the wagon, arms crossed, watching the sun dip lower in the sky. It would be sunset soon. That's when they'd find the flowering almond.

"It must be magic," Almas murmured.

Ziva said, "What is?"

"Finding a tree exactly at sunset," he said. "Because how would that little boy know how fast we'd travel? Or if we'd stop to eat, or whatever else. That seems like magic to me. It's part of a ritual to open the way to Luz. I bet if we had come from a different direction or at a different time of day, we'd never find the path."

"Are you saying that little boy is magic?" she asked.

Almas said, "No. But he knows about magic somehow. Maybe the whole tribe knows about the ritual to get to Luz, but he was the only one who would tell you."

"Maybe," Ziva said, but that didn't feel right to her. She watched the sun dip toward the horizon.

Yet another sunset drawing closer made Ziva's stomach churn. Two days was turning into one, and she didn't know how long the tunnel would take, or how far beyond it Luz lay.

But what had Chichäk said? The spirit of Death would give Pesah more time, but only long enough to arrive at the city.

The little Asena boy had said humankind had five fingers, because one wouldn't be enough.

Ziva hadn't wondered then, but she wondered now: could Chichäk's spirit be the same as Ziva's Angel of Death? Were they the same finger? And if so, why would the Angel of Death grant Pesah an extension? Why would he allow Pesah to make it to the city where he couldn't enter?

Then: if Chichäk could bargain with the spirit of Death, did that mean it would be possible for Ziva to do the same with the Angel of Death?

The thought made Ziva shudder. Bargain with the Angel of Death. She remembered his presence at the campsite nearly a month ago, and heard Avag and Petros screaming all over again. The rolling eyes embedded in shadow, the wings, the hissing sword . . .

Ziva wouldn't be able to stand upright in that thing's presence, let alone bargain with it. That must have been why Chichäk enlisted a spirit to help her bargain: so she didn't have to face Death by herself.

Ziva looked up at the top of the wagon, where the raven still perched. As she looked at it, it cocked its head to look down at her. When the raven had showed up at Chichäk's tent, one of the guards had called it a spirit. Were all ravens spirits, then? Or just some of them? Was the one perched on top of their wagon a spirit? If it was, why were spirits bringing her brother gifts?

She looked back down, tracking the bare path the horses were following. They weren't spirits. They were just weird birds.

The sun continued to set, and they kept on going north, and Ziva scoured the path ahead for an almond tree and a cavern. She didn't see anything, even though the sun was fat and low and red, and she was starting to wonder if that Asena boy had sent them on a wild chase up here.

A raven flew past, cawing, and dropped something into the opening. They were getting good at fly-by dropoffs now, and Pesah was getting good at catching the gifts.

What he caught wasn't a small coin or bit of shiny treasure, like normal. It was a little oblong brown nut. Pesah held it out to Ziva as Almas pulled the horses to a stop, eyes wide and staring.

Ziva said, "What's wrong?" as she followed Almas's gaze, and then she saw it.

A tree covered in soft pink blooms, its roots piercing the rock that hung over a cave mouth. Behind the tree, the setting sun blazed red and orange like fire, and the tree's pink blossoms were tinted with the light of the dying day.

From behind her, Pesah whispered, "Is that it?"

Almas said, "I think so."

Ziva squinted at the tree, at the sun behind it. "That's not right."

"What?" Almas asked.

Ziva pointed at the mountain peaks. "This is east, right?"

"Yes," Almas said.

"Then the sun should be over there," she said, pointing away from the mountains, toward the west. "The sun doesn't set in the east."

The three of them were silent for a while, pondering the backwards sky, and then Pesah said, "Almas mentioned a ritual, right? Maybe this tells us we did it right."

"Or wrong," Ziva mumbled.

"We did it right," Almas said.

"Should we go in now?" Pesah asked.

"Yes," Ziva said, at the same time that Almas said, "No."

They looked at one another, and Ziva scowled.

"Ziva, we should rest," Almas said.

Ziva shook her head. "It's right there," she said. "We go in, and we're safe."

Almas sighed. "This is just like the time way back when I first found you, after Avag and Petros died. You wanted to just go and go and run us all into the ground. We have two days. We have time to rest."

"We don't know how long that tunnel is!" Ziva argued. "What if it's three days long?"

Almas let out a long, slow breath. "Then we're already too late."

He let that sentiment hang in the air between them, and Ziva glared at him until Pesah said, "I'm tired. And I think the horses should get a chance to rest and eat before we go in."

Now Ziva glared at Pesah. "Whose side are you on, any-way?"

Pesah shrugged. "The horses'."

Ziva scowled some more as Almas jumped off the wagon and unhitched the horses so they could graze. She sat with her arms crossed and let him set up the camp until Pesah put his hand on her shoulder and said, "He's right to stop."

She snapped, "What if we don't make it now? What if we're too late, and you die in the back of this wagon, and then I have to—"

"It's not Rosh Hashanah," he said.

"It will be soon," Ziva said. She had never dreaded the holy day as much as she did right then. "It'll be Rosh Hashanah before you realize."

And then the Angel of Death would be there, cutting through Pesah like he had Avag and Petros, and Pesah would scream like they had, and Ziva . . .

Ziva would have to watch.

She squeezed her eyes shut and pushed off the bench. "I'm going to find water," she mumbled before jumping off the wagon and fleeing her brother.

THIRTY-SIX

THEY RESTED LIKE PESAH WANTED, even though Ziva was up before the sun and packing the wagon back up before Almas or Pesah woke. She had already hitched the horses into their traces as Almas rose, yawned, stretched, and said, "So, do I have time to make breakfast, or—"

"No," Ziva said. She spun her finger in the air. "Get up, get up. Let's go."

Almas shook his head as he climbed to his feet and stretched again, regarding the cavern mouth. "Is the wagon going to fit in there?"

"I don't know," Ziva said. She hoped so. "It looks big enough."

He tilted his head to the side. "I guess. I hope it doesn't get smaller in there, or we'll have to leave the wagon."

Ziva frowned. If they left the wagon, one of them would have to carry Pesah, since Ziva had left his chair behind. That would slow them down even more.

Almas wandered close to the cavern as Ziva roused Pesah. He coughed as he sat up, and when her fingers flitted across his forehead, he was hot again. He looked ragged, like he hadn't slept well, and after he stopped coughing he said, "I don't feel good, Ziva."

"We're almost there," she said softly, and helped him to his feet.

"We should get some wood to make torches," Almas called, squinting into the cavern. "I can't see any light, or an end on the other side. It just keeps going."

Ziva grumbled, "Fine." Another thing to slow them down, delay their journey. But as she looked into the darkness of the tunnel, her skin prickled. A dark cavern that was who-knows-how-long, with no light to make their way by, and unknown creatures within.

Almas and Ziva gathered tree branches that could be used as torches, but Pesah found an oil lamp, wicks, and a clay vessel of oil that the Asena had given them.

They brought the wood anyway, just in case, but filled the lamp and lit the wick to use as light.

"I'll walk in front of the horses," Almas said. "Lead the way with the lamp."

Ziva nodded. "Okay."

"Hey, don't be scared," Almas said. "We'll get through."

"I'm not scared," Ziva said.

Almas made a face that Ziva knew meant he didn't believe her: lifting up both his eyebrows and pursing his lips while he narrowed his eyes.

He said, "Of course you're not scared. Me neither." And then he walked up to the cave mouth with the oil lamp held aloft, turning back as Ziva climbed onto the wagon bench. "Ready?"

"Ready," she said, and urged the horses forward. The horses walked up to the cavern but wouldn't go further until Almas took one horse's bridle and pulled her into the cavern.

The wagon fit. Barely. But it fit. Once they were inside, away from the sunlight, the candle's meager flame was all they had, and as they delved deeper, Ziva heard the forlorn, farewell croak of a raven from behind them.

THIRTY-SEVEN

THE WAGON BLOCKED OUT MUCH of the light, and it only took a couple of minutes of walking for the cavern to be entirely dark. Almas talked in low, reassuring words to the horses, coaxing them forward, and Ziva gripped the reins. She watched the light of Almas's lamp bob in the darkness before her. Sometimes the side or top of the wagon would scrape against the cavern, and Ziva's heart would seize in her chest. If the tunnel got much narrower, the wagon wouldn't fit. They'd never make it to Luz on time.

Pesah shifted beside her. "I wonder if this is what leaving Egypt was like."

"Egypt," Ziva murmured. The Ninth Plague: casting Egypt into darkness. Three days of darkness. She hoped they weren't in this tunnel for three days. She could barely make him out, so she reached over and patted the top of his head. It was hot, even in the coolness of the tunnel. "I can see you, though. So it's not like Egypt."

Pesah was contemplatively quiet. "After the darkness, the next plague was . . . the firstborn."

Ziva scoffed in the darkness. "*I'm* the firstborn."

"I know," Pesah said. "You'd better watch out." He laughed, but it wasn't full and deep like his laughs usually were. It was soft and unsure.

Ziva let her hand drop from the top of Pesah's head. She fumbled, searching, until she found his bandaged fingers. She squeezed softly. "Well, we haven't done anything to cause plagues. So I don't think I have anything to worry about."

Pesah remained silent. The wagon continued on, Almas leading the horses through the darkness. They hadn't gotten stuck yet. Hopefully their luck would hold out.

Then, so softly Ziva almost didn't hear him, Pesah said, "I'm afraid, Ziva."

She squeezed his hand tighter, wishing she could see him. "We're going to make it. I promise."

Pesah took a deep breath and said, "That's not what I'm afraid of."

Ziva's heart skipped a beat, but before she could ask him what he *was* afraid of, Almas yelped, and the cavern went dark.

"Almas!" Ziva yelled. The cavern was entirely dark. She couldn't see her own hand in front of her face, let alone what was happening to Almas. Had some cavern creature jumped on him? Was he okay? Why had the lamp gone out? The darkness was suffocating, a physical weight she could feel pressing into her skin. Her stuttering heart felt crushed by that weight, unable to beat normally. And her lungs couldn't breathe in that heavy darkness. She was getting dizzy . . . or was it just that she had no frame of reference for which way was up and which was down?

Almas's voice cut through the darkness. "I dropped the lamp."

Ziva blew out a breath. He was okay.

But.

"How are we going to light it again?" she asked.

"I think it's still got oil in it," Almas said. "And I have the tinder in my pocket, but I can't light it and hold the horses. Can you come out here and hold them?"

"Of course." Ziva grasped the side of the wagon bench and lowered herself carefully to the ground. She turned to walk towards where she thought Almas was, but then realized she didn't know where he was. If she started walking away from the path, she might fall into a hole or something. Then she'd be lost forever. "Almas, say something."

"Something."

"Ha ha," she scowled. "Talk so I can get to you."

"I'm talking so you can get to me," Almas said. "Talking, talking, talking."

Ziva shuffled toward him, hands out in front of her. She felt one horse's flank as Almas continued to babble about things, and she made it to what sounded like being right next to him. But she couldn't feel him.

"Almas," Ziva said, and as she said it, his fingers touched hers. His fingers closed tightly around hers, hand warm and steady, and Ziva felt a flush heat her face and neck. He pulled her closer.

"Here," he said, and a rough rope filled her palm. "The reins."

"Oh," Ziva said. She took the reins, glad the cavern was so dark to hide her blush. Almas fumbled around, and Ziva imagined him pulling the tinder out of his pocket. The rough sound of him striking it cut through the darkness as sparks leapt up, lighting the pitch for a second before fading away. Almas struck the tinder twice more, and then the lamp caught. It glowed as Almas tucked the tinder back in his pocket. The lamp threw shadows up around his face, making his features look twisted. In the dancing light of the flame, surrounded by nothing but blackness, he looked rightly demonic.

And then he held the lamp up, so it could spread its light further, and he didn't look like a demon anymore. Ziva surprised herself just then with a wish said silently: she hoped he didn't leave once they all got to Luz.

He took the reins from her. "You can go back up with Pesah. Thanks for helping me."

Ziva nodded. "Why don't I stay? Keep helping. I can lead the horses."

"You should rest," Almas said. "Plus, I know you don't like the dark."

"I've rested enough." Ziva took the reins from Almas's hand. "And you're right. I don't like the dark. But it's not dark up here with you."

Almas's face shifted into a careful smile. "Well, all right." He went ahead, lamp lighting a tiny path through the tunnel, and Ziva followed carefully behind. The only sounds in the cavern were their own footsteps on the ground, the occasional scraping of the wagon on the walls or ceiling, and the horses' breaths in and out.

Almas said, "How long have we been in here?"

Ziva didn't know. It felt like it had been days. Weeks. Years. An eternity. Like the sun was a myth she'd only heard about from elders. "Forever."

He laughed. "Why are you afraid of the dark?"

"Who said I'm afraid?" Ziva snapped. But then she bit the end of her tongue, sighed, and said, "Fine. I'm afraid."

Almas turned, glancing at her with a soft frown. "I don't blame you. There are dangerous things in the dark."

"It's not that," Ziva said. "Back when . . . when Pesah first got sick. It wasn't all of a sudden he went from healthy to sick, you know. It's been years. At first he had these little white patches on his arms and his face."

She was glad it was too dark for her to look at the patch on her own skin.

She continued: "And then he couldn't feel things anymore. His hands got all hurt. Like, he'd cut himself and not even feel it. We wouldn't know until there was blood everywhere."

Almas was silent, listening and taking careful steps through the tunnel.

"We always slept in the same room," Ziva said. "We were never apart. I could wake up any time at night and hear him breathing on the other side of the room, and I'd know he was safe. I've always made sure Pesah was safe. But then Uncle Sabriel came and said Pesah shouldn't be in my room anymore. That he might make me sick. So they moved him into his own room. Then his own house. And—"

And her voice scraped against the sides of her throat the way the wagon scraped against the sides of the tunnel. But unlike the wagon, her voice got caught, stuck, lodged there. Her hands on the reins trembled, and her eyes burned. She was glad for the darkness then, to hide her tears from Almas, to hide the emotion she couldn't swallow away.

Almas stayed quiet. He gave her the time she needed to dislodge her voice.

"And when I'd wake up at night, I couldn't hear him breathing," Ziva said softly. "I didn't know if he was alive, or . . ." She sniffed. "So I'd just have to lie there in the darkness and think. Think about Pesah's sickness. Think about what I heard Uncle Sabriel tell Baba when they thought I couldn't hear. Think about how my mother didn't hug Pesah anymore. Think about his . . . his funeral. What he'd look like when they buried him. How far the disease would have eaten him away."

She was whispering at the end, tears rolling down her cheeks and dropping off to wet the dusty tunnel floor.

"So," she said, sniffling. "I'm afraid of the dark. But not because I think there are monsters in it. I don't care about monsters. The dark is when I can't be with Pesah. When I don't know if he's alive still, or if the disease took him. The dark means that if Pesah dies, he'll die alone."

And if Pesah died, Ziva would be alone, too. They would each be without the other. They'd never been alone in their lives; not really. They'd never done something without the other one there. Even birth. They'd come into the world together, but Pesah's illness had forced Ziva to face the knowledge that they would very likely leave the world far, far apart.

Almas slowed so he could walk by Ziva's side, and he wrapped one arm around her. He pulled her close, squeezed her in a hug, and then released. He didn't say anything. He didn't need to.

THIRTY-EIGHT

ZIVA WALKED WITH ALMAS until her feet started to get sore, and then he insisted she go rest. She did, carefully finding her way back to the wagon so she could sit on the bench again. Pesah was inside, sleeping, but he woke up when she said his name.

"Welcome back," Pesah said, yawning.

"I wanted to help Almas out," she said.

"Of course," Pesah said. "How long have we been in here?"

"Forever," Ziva said. She didn't say what she feared: that it was already Rosh Hashanah, and that they'd round a corner and run smack into the Angel of Death blocking their way.

Then, they did round a corner, and Almas's lamp glowed brighter.

"What the—" Ziva mumbled, squinting. Had he pulled the wick up somehow to make the flame bigger? But it would have been the whole wick. It was too bright. Almost as bright as—

"Ziva!" Almas shouted, pointing, laughing.

Sunshine.

The end of the tunnel was bright, a searing white. Midday sun at least. The horses picked up their pace, hurrying toward it, and Almas let them pass and jumped on the bench with Ziva.

Ziva had never appreciated the sun more than she did then, as the wagon trundled out of the tunnel. She nearly tumbled over the front of the bench, she was leaning out so far. Almas had his face turned toward the light, eyes shut, mouth open as he inhaled.

"I thought—" His voice cracked, and he cleared his throat. "I thought we'd never see it again."

Ziva nodded, and Pesah reached his hand out of the wagon door. His bandaged fingers lit up in the sunlight. Ziva met his eyes with hers, and they both laughed with relief.

The wagon stopped.

Ziva turned away from Pesah to look at why the horses had stopped. Almas clung tightly to the reins, his eyes wide as he looked out before them. Ziva followed his gaze, heart thumping even before she saw what was before them, even before Almas whispered.

"A red land."

The land was indeed red, but it looked strange. Lumpy. Variegated. The road cut through the strange redness, going east, until it ended at a city with high, blue walls standing in the distance.

"Luz," Ziva breathed. It had to be. "Almas, go."

"But . . ." He swung his arm forward. "A red land. A blue road through a red land. That's where Pesah's going to—"

"He won't if you hurry," Ziva snapped. It wasn't Rosh Hashanah yet. It wouldn't start until sunset, hours away. They had time. "So hurry."

Almas hesitated, but then slapped the reins. The horses pulled, snorting, as they marched along the road, and Ziva squinted at the red earth on either side of them.

But it wasn't the earth that was red.

Apples. Thousands and thousands of apples, littering the ground on either side of the road, as far as Ziva could see in either direction. The horses looked at the apples, then tossed their heads and kept toward the city.

Almas frowned. "The horses don't even want to eat them."

"Why are they here?" Ziva asked.

No one said anything for a while, and then Pesah said, "The garden."

Ziva turned to look at him. "What?"

"The story of the Milcham," Pesah said. "Remember? It was the only creature in the garden that didn't eat the apple."

The three of them contemplated the thousands of apples, still red and shining, piled up on either side of the road.

Then Ziva asked, "How long have they been here, do you think?"

Almas shrugged. "They all look fresh. Like they just fell off a tree."

"They can't have all *just* fallen off a tree," Ziva said. First of all, there were no trees anywhere. Second, it would have taken thousands of trees all dropping their apples at the same time, and Ziva didn't think that would ever happen.

"I bet you can't get into the city if you have apples," Pesah said. "So travelers who come here have to leave their apples on the side of the road. And they've been doing that for hundreds and hundreds of years."

Almas's frown deepened, and Ziva said, "But why aren't they rotten, then?"

"Why is the sun going the wrong way?" Pesah said, pointing at the sky. "I don't know. Maybe the city's magic extends out here . . . Maybe it keeps them from rotting."

Ziva nodded. Something was keeping them fresh, and Pesah's explanation was as good as any Ziva could think of.

The sun shone bright as it made its backwards descent behind Luz, throwing the city's shadow over the apples and the road. The wagon approached a crossroads, even though the other roads were covered up with apples so only the one was passable. An enormous boulder sat off to the side of the road itself, marked with etchings and scratches and charcoal. Next to it, a little pond reflected the bright blue of the sky.

Someone was sitting on the boulder, facing the city, tossing small stones into the pond.

The horses came to a stop.

Ziva hissed at Almas, "Keep going!"

"I didn't stop them," he said, voice shaking. He slapped the reins and clicked his tongue, but the horses didn't move.

And then Ziva heard the hissing.

She thought it was a snake at first. A cobra, perhaps. There had been a man at the market in Atil a couple summers ago, and he'd brought a cobra in a basket, and the snake had risen out and hissed at the man, but hadn't tried to bite him. That's what Ziva heard now: the deadly, angry threat of something menacing. Something that wasn't allowed to bite, but desperately wanted to.

She whispered, "Do you hear that?"

"Hear what?" Almas whispered.

From behind her, Pesah whispered, "Yes."

"Almas, go," Ziva said.

He slapped the horses with the reins again. They didn't move. "I can't."

The person sitting on the crossroads stone stopped throwing the pebbles into the pond, sat still for a moment, and then stood. Ziva clapped her hands over her mouth to keep the scream in. He was tiny himself, the size of a child, but his shadow was huge along the ground. The shadow had wings, and burning eyes, and a sword that hissed and seethed.

She looked up from the shadow that crawled toward them, falling over the apples as they crumbled into black dust.

She knew him.

And he knew her.

"Angels are good," the Asena boy said in a small voice. "Even the Angel of Death."

THIRTY-NINE

THE ASENA BOY.

The one with the baklava.

He stood on the stone, an enormous, frothing sword clutched casually in one hand, its tip hanging off the side of the boulder and dripping poison onto the ground.

He was the Angel of Death. He was *malach ha-mavet*, offering her sweets. Her mouth was sour, dry, gummed up, and she was so, so glad she hadn't taken the baklava from him.

At the Asena camp, he had asked her if angels were good, and she had said yes. And then he'd asked, *Even the Angel of Death?* And she hadn't said yes.

Death is good sometimes, she had said. *But not for Pesah.*

Ziva lunged to the side, grabbed the reins from Almas, and she screamed, "Not for Pesah!"

Then she slapped the reins and yelled, "Hyah!" as loudly as she could, and the horses bolted forward so suddenly that Ziva fell onto Almas. He yelped and grabbed onto her, then onto the bench, and the reins went flying but the horses kept running. Ziva felt herself propelled toward the edge of the bench, off the side, and she swallowed a scream as she braced herself for a hard fall. But Almas's arm was there, looped around her, holding her in the wagon as the horses bolted to the city.

The Angel of Death followed.

He didn't fly or float or anything like that. He walked, taking long strides like a little boy keeping up with his father. One step, and he had passed the crossroads. Two steps, and he covered the distance of ten strides for a normal man.

Ziva's fingers gripped the bench so hard she could feel the wood under her nails. The sword dragged behind the Angel of Death, leaving a long gouge in the dirt of the road.

He took another step. He was halfway to them.

But they were almost to the city. They were going to make it.

They were going to make it.

But . . .

The horses were slowing down.

Ziva turned to look back at the horses, to try to grab the reins and make them go faster again, but they weren't slowing down on purpose. They were running in slow motion, like they were moving through thick syrup, struggling against some invisible force that was slowing them. As they got closer to the city, they became even slower.

"What's happening?" Ziva yelled.

"I don't know!" Almas said.

From within the wagon, Pesah yelled, "Ziva!"

She hurried inside, scrambling, terrified that the Angel of Death had somehow gotten inside and was killing Pesah as they struggled to get into the city. The angel wasn't there, though. Just Pesah, digging through all the supplies the Asena had given them.

"Pesah," Ziva said. "What—"

"Apples!" Pesah yelled. "We can't go into the city if we have apples!"

Ziva stood, unsure what to do for a moment. Apples . . . was that really it? Where did they have apples in here? They hadn't gotten fresh fruit in almost a week.

But . . . what if the Asena had gifted them some?

Ziva dropped to her knees and started doing what Pesah was doing—emptying out bags and boxes—only faster. Because she had all her fingers. The white spot on her wrist caught her eye, mocked her.

She had all her fingers . . . *for now.*

Ziva stopped being careful and just started flinging boxes around, tipping bags entirely upside-down to allow their contents to pour out.

Bread. Figs. Dried meat. Dried apricots. No apples. There were no apples. Ziva dug through the piles already on the floor, fingers shaking. There had to be some apples somewhere. Maybe dried apples in a small sack? Apple seeds in something? Apple juice hidden in one of the skeins. Something. *Anything.*

Pesah emptied a sack and a pair of apples rolled out, two shiny red stowaways that bumped against Ziva's shoes.

She stared at them, heart leaping into her mouth for half a breath before she snatched them up. She darted out the front of the wagon, then turned, facing backwards, and hurled the first apple over the top of the wagon.

The apple barely missed the Asena boy. The Angel of Death. He was perched on top of the wagon like the ravens had been over the past weeks. The sword gripped in his hand hissed, spat poison, sucked air and light from the space around itself.

The boy smiled at her. "Are you ready?"

Ziva ground her teeth together and spat, "Not today."

Then she threw the second apple.

It bent around *malach ha-mavet* and vanished into the air behind him. As soon as it left her fingers, the horses surged forward. Ziva yelped as she slammed face-first against the wagon wall, then fell backwards onto the bench. Almas had found the reins and gripped them as the syrupy slowness disappeared, and the wagon careened into the city of Luz.

PART FOUR

The city of Luz.

They had made it.

As soon as they crossed the threshold into the city, things changed. The world *lifted*. Any aches or pains from the journey were gone. Ziva's thirst and hunger evaporated. And Pesah . . . Pesah pushed up on his own.

They had made it, gentle listener.

But . . . at what cost?

FORTY

ZIVA, PESAH, AND ALMAS SCREAMED as the wagon careened into the city. The horses jammed their front hooves down to slow themselves as Almas yanked the reins back, and Ziva yelled, "Stop! Stop!"

"I'm trying!" Almas yelled back at her.

Pesah just clung to the wagon's opening, eyes screwed shut.

Finally, the horses came to a stop. Ziva scrambled up, looking back to make sure they hadn't hurt anyone.

The street was empty. Beyond it, standing outside the gate beyond the threshold, the Angel of Death lingered. He was staring straight at Ziva. Still smiling.

Triumph surged in Ziva's chest. They had made it. They had beaten him, Death himself, into the city, and now Pesah would live. She was tempted to make a rude gesture at the Angel of Death, but before she could decide on one, he turned. He walked away, and the city gates swung shut of their own accord.

Almas watched the Angel of Death go too, and then he turned slowly to Ziva. "We made it."

She nodded, breathing hard. "We made it."

Almas looked around. "Where is everyone?"

"I don't know," Ziva said. The emptiness was worrying. She didn't know what she had expected here, but an uninhabited city was not it.

Pesah coughed from inside the wagon, and Ziva's heart sank. He sounded the same. She lowered herself to the bench beside him and patted him on the back.

He looked up at her with watering eyes, coughing behind his bandages, and between fits he managed to whisper to her, "I'm still sick, Ziva. This place hasn't changed that."

Ziva's elation at escaping Death dulled, and she said nothing. He was sick, sure. But they'd get to the Milcham. They'd get a feather and cure Pesah's leprosy and his cough and everything. Once the coughing fit subsided, Ziva took the reins and said, "Let's go find someone. Find the king, or the Milcham bird."

Almas and Pesah nodded, and Ziva gently urged the horses forward. The cobblestone streets were spotlessly clean, and the little stucco buildings were painted a heavenly blue, with golden stars over the doorways. A pleasant scent, like cinnamon and fresh bread, permeated the air. The sun was softer here, friendlier. Warm but not hot.

They turned a corner, and Ziva pulled the horses to a stop. There, massed in the road like a festival crowd, was what looked like the population of the entire city. They all faced the wagon, and when they saw Ziva, Almas, and Pesah, they sent up a great cheer that made the horses startle a little.

An old man hurried up to the wagon and said, "Welcome, welcome!"

Ziva couldn't help but grin. "Hello!"

The man bowed with his hand on his chest. "My name is Ekrem. Welcome to Luz!"

"I'm Ziva." She offered the man a head nod in return, and motioned to Almas and Pesah as she said their names.

Ekrem grinned as his eyes shifted from Ziva to Almas to Pesah. They lingered on Pesah for a few beats, and then he said, "What were you dying of, young man?"

Pesah shifted and cleared his throat. "Leprosy."

Ekrem nodded. "I see. What a tragedy, what a tragedy. Well, you're here now. No Death allowed in the city!" He clapped. "As long as you stay here, you'll live long!"

The crowd cheered and chanted, "Live long! Live long!"

Ziva laughed and looked over at Almas, shouting so she could be heard over the crowd's cheers. "Did you know it would be like this?"

He laughed. "No! Hey, remember, we need the Milcham's feather if we want to cure Pesah and leave."

"I remember," Ziva said. She shouted, "Ekrem! Excuse me, Ekrem!"

He was dancing about, waving his hands in the air and chanting, "Live long!" So it took Ziva a moment to get his attention. When she did, he was beaming and rosy.

"We need to see the Milcham," Ziva said to Ekrem.

"Of course, of course," Ekrem said. "Everyone sees the Milcham!"

Ziva let out a breath of relief. Somewhere inside, she'd harbored the fear that the Milcham wouldn't be real, or it wouldn't see visitors. But neither of those things were true. It was real. And they would see it. And it would grant Pesah a feather, and then they'd be able to go back to Atil. Would Almas come with them, or would he go somewhere else to be a baker? She surprised herself with the intensity of her wish that he'd come to Atil with them.

Ziva waited for Ekrem to lead them to the Milcham, or at least tell them where to go. But he just swayed, dancing in an old-man way, until she said, "Ekrem? Where's the Milcham?"

He pointed toward the center of the city. "The Milcham waits in the palace!"

"And we just go there?" Ziva asked.

"You just go there."

"We don't need to be announced or anything?" she asked.

Ekrem laughed. "Announced for what? He already knows you're here."

That knowledge should have made Ziva happy, but instead a chill wound its way across her skin. She rubbed her palms across her arms to make the gooseflesh go away, and then she said, "Thank you, Ekrem." And she turned the horses in the direction Ekrem had indicated. In the distance, towering over the little blue houses, was an enormous wall looping around something in the center. That must have been the palace.

The sounds of the party faded as they drew nearer to the wall. It was painted blue like the rest of the buildings, accented by gold stars here and there.

Ziva reined in the horses to stop before a gap in the wall. A tall archway led in, and beyond it, all Ziva could make out were lush plants.

She looked over at Pesah. "Are you ready?"

He nodded. "I think so."

"How about you, Almas?" Ziva asked.

Almas was staring at the archway, the wall. He looked at Ziva with a worried expression. "Yeah. I guess."

"Great," Ziva said. They were about to meet the Milcham. To gain life for Pesah. To return home and live normally again.

To defeat Death, once and for all.

FORTY-ONE

PESAH COUGHED AS HE GOT DOWN from the wagon. He wobbled on weak, twisted ankles, grasping onto the wagon bench for balance.

Ziva watched him with a held breath. He was still coughing. His legs were still twisted. His bandages were all still there.

She shook her head. The Milcham would help. It could take away his cough and his inability to walk and his scars. It could make Pesah whole again.

Pesah's bandages were creased in a way that, Ziva knew, meant he was frowning. "I can't stand."

"It hurts too much?" Ziva asked. Of course it did. It always had.

"No," he said. "It doesn't hurt anymore. Just . . . I'm too weak, I think."

Almas slid down from the other side and came around, extending his arm to Pesah. "Does this help?"

Pesah nodded and took Almas's arm, gripping it carefully. The three of them looked up at the wall, the arch, and the garden beyond.

Ziva went in first. The tall archway's edges were painted gold, like the stars, shining in the sunlight. She looked up at the sparkling gold for a moment, and then directed her eyes down. She tried to find the palace that Ekrem had spoken of, but all she could see was a garden. It was lush, thick, and quiet. The trees were enormous, casting the entire place into peaceful shadow.

She hesitated. "Didn't Ekrem say there was a palace?"

Almas said, "I think so."

"Okay." Ziva continued stepping forward. "It must be past all the trees."

The garden had a tiny whisper of a path that wound in, so Ziva followed that. Almas and Pesah followed behind. They went deeper into the garden, and even though it had all the makings of a peaceful place, the hairs on the back of Ziva's neck stood up.

Some of the plants Ziva recognized. She spotted some almonds, apricots, figs, and dates between other plants that were foreign to her. Every tree or bush or vine had fruit or flowers on it. Here and there, long shimmering feathers had been discarded on the ground, like a flock of shining birds had just been there. They passed a fountain, painted blue with gold stars, and paused near it.

Ziva squinted up the path. "I don't see a palace. At all. How big is this garden?"

"It can't be *that* big," Pesah said. "The city itself isn't that big."

"Well, there's no palace in here," Ziva said. "Maybe we should go back out. Maybe we came to the wrong place."

"Maybe," Pesah agreed.

But Almas shook his head. "No. It's here."

Ziva looked back at him. His head was cocked, eyes wide and darting from treetop to treetop. Ziva followed his gaze toward the sky, and she saw a large shape, concealed in shadow, sliding from tree to tree.

"Almas," she whispered, grabbing onto his arm.

Pesah looked up too, and Almas said, "I think that's the Milcham."

"I hope so," Pesah said. "Because if it's not . . ."

Ziva finished for him in her head. *Because if it's not the Milcham, then what is it?*

They watched the shape climb down the tree. It came closer and the shadows faded away, revealing feathers that shimmered in the dappled light that fell on them. The creature reached the base of the tree and alit upon the ground, then marched toward the trio.

"Well," it said in a voice like scraping rocks together. "Well, well."

Ziva couldn't do anything but stare. It was as tall as Baba, maybe taller, with a man's bearded face. It didn't have a man's eyes, though, but the intense golden eyes of a bird of prey. From the chin down, it was a bird. A beautiful, colorful bird with riotous blues and golds catching every mote of light and reflecting it out. It had a long tail—not like a peacock, but thin and straight. It stretched out its wings, which spanned all the way from one side of the fountain clearing to the other.

It flapped its wings a time or two and then tucked them back against its body. "I am the Milcham."

Almas bowed his head, and Pesah followed suit. Ziva did as well, heart thumping in her chest. "My name is Ziva. This is my brother, Pesah, and our friend Almas."

The Milcham scrutinized Almas, then turned to Pesah. "You have come to seek shelter."

Pesah nodded. "Yes, I have, please."

The Milcham rustled its feathers. "I saw you in the tunnel. I prepared a home in case you made it. You are granted your shelter for eternity."

"Thank you," Pesah said, bowing again.

The Milcham said, "And your friends, too." It blinked long at Almas. "I suppose."

Ziva cleared her throat and said, "Um, excuse me? We were wondering if . . . well, we'd heard that your feathers can heal the sick or infirm."

The Milcham looked at her, and she regretted speaking up. Its gaze was searing hot, like someone was holding a flame to her skin. "You heard correctly."

"Oh!" Relief flooded Ziva. This was happening. This was about to happen. She could see Pesah in her mind, unscarred, whole, walking on his own. Just the thought of it made her chest tight. "Well, we were wondering if my brother—Pesah, his name is Pesah—if he could have a feather and be healed."

The Milcham blinked at her. "No."

The warmth in Ziva sizzled out into coldness. Her tentative smile dropped off her face. "What? Why?"

The Milcham ruffled its feathers again. "Because I did that before, long ago, and people would leave. They would die. Outside is death. Do you know why there is death?"

Ziva did know. She remembered the road to the city, the red land all around it. "Because of the apple."

"Because of the *apple*," the Milcham repeated in a hiss. "Because the others wanted to *know* things. Well, Milcham didn't want to *know anything*. And my reward is to live forever, but the others . . ." It shook its head slowly. "Death, death, death. And the sick ones who come here not to live but to be healed will die anyway, because Death is hungry. And cruel. He doesn't care for cures or health. He will take a person anyway." The Milcham snapped its teeth at Ziva. "So no. No cures. No healing. Only staying here. You will be comfortable. And alive. You will be alive."

"What about me and Almas?" Ziva asked. "We're not sick. Can we leave?" Not that she would. If she left Luz, she would leave Pesah. And hadn't this whole journey been so she wouldn't have to be without him?

The Milcham paced, putting one scaly bird foot in front of the other. "Death cares not for health. Cares not for health. You will die out there. Stay here. Stay safe."

"But—"

The Milcham squawked before Ziva could finish. It sounded angry, and the way it glared at her seemed angry too. It spread out its wings and leapt into the air, disappearing over the treetops a moment later.

FORTY-TWO

THEY LEFT THE GARDEN. Ziva's mind swirled with frustration and anxiety, but she couldn't arrange words in any sort of coherent way. No cures. No healing. Only suspended life. She couldn't look at Pesah, because whenever she did, her guilt tore at her with claws. She had dragged him all the way here, and for what? To live scarred and unable to walk without assistance, far away from their home.

And Almas . . . he had agreed to bring them here, and now he was freed of his promise to her. But could he leave now? Or would the Angel of Death meet him at the gates, sword slashing, ready to take him?

She looked down at the ground, passing by those feathers they'd walked past on the way in. She stooped and picked up three vibrant feathers. If the Milcham wouldn't gift them any, then she'd take some.

Pesah noticed. "Are you stealing magic feathers?"

"No," Ziva said. "I'm tidying them up."

Pesah pinned her with an incredulous stare. *"Ziva."*

"What? Pesah, it's a mess in here," she said. "He should thank me for picking up after him."

As they exited the garden, Ekrem greeted them. He was standing by the horses, patting each on the nose with a hand, and Ziva caught herself wondering if the horses were doomed to stay here forever, too, and if she should grab two extra feathers for them.

Ekrem grinned at Ziva. "You met him. Isn't he wonderful?"

She could think of a whole slew of words that she'd use to describe the Milcham other than "wonderful." Instead, she said, "He said we can stay here."

"Oh yes, yes." Ekrem clapped his hands softly. "I'll show you. Whoops!" He laughed and plucked the feathers out of her hand. "Those have to stay in the garden."

Ziva reached for the feathers, but pulled her hand away before she looked like she was trying to steal them back. "Oh. Uh. Really? They're so pretty, though. Can't we keep them as, um, decoration?"

"They certainly are beautiful," Ekrem said. "But no, my dear; no, I'm afraid." He skipped over to the garden's closest gate and lobbed the feathers inside, where they drifted in tight spirals to the ground. "There! All set. Let's get going, hm?"

Ziva stared at the lost feathers as she helped Almas maneuver Pesah onto the bench, and before she could make room for Ekrem, he was off, walking briskly down the road. Ziva and Almas scrambled into the wagon and urged the horses after him. He led them through the city's winding streets, yapping the whole way.

"Oh, Luz, such a blessing to have," Ekrem said. "I came here a long time ago. When? I don't remember. I came here because I was turning old and weak, and I didn't want to die. No one wants to die, you know? And my son said to me, 'Father, there's a city to the east, and you can live forever.' So I sought this place out, and I've been here ever since. I haven't seen my son, but I know that he's happy for me." Ekrem smiled up at them.

Pesah said, "I'm sure he's very happy."

Ekrem nodded. "Of course he is." They passed a large square with dozens of people in it. "Ah, the festival!"

Ziva said, "For Rosh Hashanah?"

"For what?" Ekrem asked, wrinkling his nose. "No. It's a festival because you've joined us! And tomorrow, we'll have a festival because the sky is blue. Parties! Festivals! Games! Every night!"

Ziva held in a groan. "Every night?"

"Of course!" Ekrem laughed. "Everyone's invited. Everyone. Every single person in the city. And they all come. We have such grand parties!"

Ziva looked over at Pesah, forcing a smile. Parties for Pesah, that he could go to, because no one here would be worried about falling ill because of him. She smiled at him, even though she didn't want to go to any stupid parties.

"Parties, Pesah," Ziva said, trying to sound as cheerful as she could. "You can go to parties again!"

Pesah nodded. "Yeah. Yeah, I can."

They came to a small home—blue, of course, like all the others—with an open spot to park the wagon, and an attached stable for the horses.

Ekrem opened the house's door. Ziva and Almas helped Pesah down, and the three of them followed Ekrem into the house. The floors were swept stone, dotted with woven rugs. There was sparse furniture. A stack of pallets they could arrange at night for sleeping. A cooking area. A dining area.

It was very small, and sterile, and . . .

Ziva hated it.

Pesah breathed hard, and when he managed to catch his breath, he said, "It's lovely, Ekrem. Thank you."

"I'm glad you like it," Ekrem said.

"I have a question," Pesah said. "Since we're here forever."

Ekrem clapped. "Forever and ever."

Pesah nodded. "Yes. Well, I love to read. And I see no bookshelves or books in here. So, how would I go about getting a bookshelf?"

Ekrem shook his head. "No need for bookshelves here. No books."

Pesah just stared at him. "I'm sorry. What?"

"No books in Luz," Ekrem said. "Who needs books when you have parties?" He spun in a circle, arms raised to the ceiling.

Pesah gaped at him, and Ziva knew the answer in his mouth before he said it: *"I do!"*

"No," Ekrem said, still smiling. "You think you do, but you don't. You don't need a lot of things here. Like books. Or food!"

Almas blanched. "There's no *food?*"

"Nope!" Ekrem said. "There's no need for food. You'll never be hungry!"

"Yeah, but . . ." Almas's mouth opened and shut wordlessly for a few breaths, and then he blurted, "Food tastes so good!"

"You won't even miss it," Ekrem assured him. He breezed over to the door and said, "At sunset, we celebrate! Be in the town square for your festival!"

And then he was gone, letting the door fall shut with a bump.

FORTY-THREE

ZIVA SAT SILENT after Ekrem's departure, and Almas paced around the room after helping Pesah sit on one of the chairs.

"No books," Pesah muttered. He looked down at his bandaged hands. "No books, Ziva. How am I supposed to research? Or learn anything? Or . . . or just have *something* to do?"

"No food," Almas muttered. "No soft challah. No savory stew. No flaky baklava. No warm—"

"Almas!" Ziva snapped. "Stop! I wasn't hungry before, but you listing off food is making me hungry now!"

Almas flailed his arms in the air. "There's no food here, Ziva!"

"I heard him," she muttered. No food. No books. What did people *do* all day? Parties, apparently. A party every day for eternity. That sounded to Ziva like torture. "I can fix this."

"How?" Almas asked, still pacing. He was chewing on a fingernail, like it would somehow taste like whatever food he needed at the moment.

"I'm going to cure Pesah with the Milcham's feather," Ziva said.

Pesah sighed. "You already tried to take some, and that didn't work."

"I know," she said. "I'm going back. I'm going to get more."

Pesah and Almas exchanged a look, and Almas said, "I don't know about that, Ziva."

"It's not fair," she said, sticking a stiff finger in the direction of the garden. "He has the ability to cure Pesah of his leprosy, but he won't do it. Because why? Because someone in the past got cured and left and died anyway. He's withholding something precious."

"What's he withholding?" Pesah asked.

"Life!" Ziva said. She motioned to the room around them. "No food. No books. No . . . anything that we love. Do you think this is living? No, Pesah. This is just . . . this is just *not dying*. He's a stupid bird-man. I don't care that he's been alive for thousands of years. He's stupid."

Pesah breathed out slowly, and Almas took the opportunity to say, "You're going to steal an immortal, magical bird's feather inside his own immortal, magical city?"

Ziva crossed her arms. "Yes."

"What about *malach ha-mavet*?" Pesah said. "The Milcham said he doesn't care about sickness or cures. That he'll take us anyway. And . . ." Pesah rubbed his arm idly. "Can you two even leave now? Now that you're here?"

"Of course we can," Ziva said, even though she wasn't entirely sure. The Milcham hadn't been very clear on that, but she thought of the Asena boy in the camp—the Asena boy who was the Angel of Death in disguise—and what he'd said.

Death waits outside the city, he had said. *And anyone who steps outside . . .* He'd snapped his fingers before running off into the darkness.

He'd warned her not to cross into Luz.

The Angel of Death himself had warned her.

But she'd ignored him.

Oh well. Too late now. They were already inside, and the only way back out was with one of the Milcham's feathers. But there were three of them, so . . .

"I'll need three feathers," Ziva said.

Almas groaned. "How do you expect to do that?"

"There were feathers just lying all over the place in there," Ziva said. "Ekrem didn't put those feathers somewhere special. He just threw them on the ground. I can wait for it to be dark, and then sneak in while the Milcham is sleeping, and just grab them up again. Then we run."

"You're assuming he sleeps," Almas said.

"Sure," Ziva said, crossing the room to the door. "It's almost sunset. I'll be back some time. Pack up and get us ready to leave, okay?"

Her hand was on the door, pushing it open, when someone knocked from the other side.

Ziva snatched her hand away, heart pounding, afraid someone had heard her talking about stealing feathers and had come to mete out justice. But when she cracked the door open, it wasn't a soldier or guard. It was Ekrem, grinning.

"Are you ready to come to the party?" he asked.

Ziva wanted to tell him to go away, but then Almas was at her side. "Are we ever!"

Ekrem clapped and turned, but didn't leave. He waited for them in front of their house.

Almas helped Pesah stand and walk to the door. He gave Ziva a heavy look. "Come on, Ziva. Party time."

She mumbled, "Fine," and followed them outside.

Ekrem led them to the streets right inside the gate where they'd first come in. The place had been dressed up for a festival, with candles and lanterns and music and laughter and dancing. No food, though. No drink.

Pesah said wistfully, "Maybe I'll learn to play an instrument."

Ziva nodded. "Maybe." But she wasn't listening to the music or watching the dancers or anything like that. She was looking around for the Milcham. She didn't see him anywhere, so she said to Ekrem, "Does the Milcham ever come to these parties?"

Ekrem shrugged. "Oh, sometimes. Not often. On special occasions."

"It's Rosh Hashanah," Ziva said. "It's special."

"So it is!" Ekrem said, turning in a little circle. "A very special night! A night of farewells and so longs!"

"What?" Ziva asked, and then the celebration lulled just a little.

A woman who looked a little older than Baba emerged from the crowd, walking slowly, shoulders thrown back, chin up. Resolute. She passed close to Ekrem, and he bowed to her. She bowed a little in return, and kept walking.

Almas whispered, "Who is she?"

Ekrem shushed him, and everyone watched in silence as she walked to the gate. Put her hand on it. And pushed it open.

Some people in the crowd gasped. A few walked away, shaking their heads. Most stayed to watch, with many clamoring to a place with a good view of her.

She stood in the open gateway for a few breaths, staring out into the falling night. Ziva did what others were doing, and shifted around so she could see clearly what was happening. Outside the gate, past the hills made of apples, sat the crossroads stone. It was empty. The Angel of Death wasn't there.

As the city watched, the woman stepped outside the gate.

Some people in the crowd gasped again. There were even a few wails.

The woman walked down the road, slowly and deliberately, and then stopped abruptly, swaying where she stood. Almost like someone was standing in front of her, speaking to her.

But wasn't someone?

Could Ziva see a small figure in front of her, backlit by an enormous winged shadow, dragging a hissing sword?

She could, but she couldn't, and before she could figure out if what she was seeing was real, the woman collapsed.

Ziva startled at the suddenness of it. The woman went down in a heap, lying motionless on the road, and the crowd inside the city writhed and moaned and wailed for her. Ziva put her hand up to cover her gaping mouth.

Ekrem shook his head, humming loudly, and then the gate swung shut. He lifted his head up and bellowed, "We celebrate her life!"

"Celebrate!" the crowd bellowed back, and the music rushed up in volume, and people were dancing again, and Ziva's chest felt squeezed by an invisible serpent. That woman had died. Were they leaving her there? They were dancing and singing and celebrating . . . but they had been going to do that anyway. Was no one going to bury her?

There was no way she'd let this happen to Pesah. She was getting him out of this city, no matter what.

Ziva turned and ran from the celebration, dodging into the dim streets, headed to the Milcham's garden.

FORTY-FOUR

ZIVA MADE IT TO THE GATE of the Milcham's garden before stopping, crouching in the shadows to catch her breath. She could see through the gate and make out the dim moonlit shimmer of feathers on the ground. Just three. She only needed to dart in, grab three, and then she and Pesah and Almas could get out of there.

She inhaled deeply a few times, inflating her courage, and then a hand grabbed her arm, and she yelped and spun around, hands up to slap away her assailant.

"Shh!" Almas hissed, crouched in the shadows right behind her.

Ziva swallowed her heart, which had leapt up into her mouth, so she could spit, "Almas, you almost scared me inside out!"

"Good," he said. "Scared enough to *not* go through with this?"

"Of course I'm going through with it," Ziva said. "Did you see what happened out there?"

"That woman died?"

"Yes," Ziva said, "But after that. They just shut the gate and forgot about her! Her body's still lying out on the road. That's . . . that's . . ." She couldn't put a word to how she felt. Disgusted and sad and angry and afraid. "I'm not letting that happen to Pesah."

Almas nodded toward the garden. "The Milcham is in there. What do you think's going to happen if it catches you stealing its feathers?"

It'd probably fling her out of the city to die. Ziva squared her jaw. "It's worth the risk."

"Ziva—"

"It is." Ziva shoved away from him, creeping toward the garden gate, ignoring Almas's hissing from behind her. She crept up to the entrance, where the city's cobbled streets turned into the lush greenery of the garden, and peered inside. All was quiet, muted. Like a blanket of silence was tucked around the whole garden. She paused, listening for the Milcham's movement through the trees. Nothing.

A feather was right there. She needed to take two steps inside the gate, and she could grab it. A second feather was just past the first, and a third lay crookedly against the base of a tree a little further in. She estimated the distance. Two steps to the first, six to the second, maybe ten to the third. Eighteen steps and she'd be done, feathers in hand, and they could escape.

"You can do it, Ziva," she whispered to herself. "Do it for Pesah."

She crossed into the garden, then paused. When the Milcham didn't descend upon her in a whirlwind of rage, she crept another step and scooped up the feather. Gripping it in sweaty fingers, she hurried to the next feather.

"Ziva!"

Almas's voice, whispering behind her, made her whirl and glare. He was at the garden gate, poking his head in but not the rest of his body. He looked extremely concerned.

She turned back, ignoring him, and snatched up the second feather.

"Ziva!"

Louder this time, and she wanted to yell for him to shut up, but she didn't. Because something was shaking the treetops in the garden.

And it was coming closer.

The third feather was ten steps away.

The treetops shook: closer, closer.

Did she have time to grab it before the Milcham got here? What would happen when he did?

She was frozen, breath trapped in her chest, panic welling up. And then she pitched forward, legs barely catching her, running to the third feather. The treetops shook, showering the garden with leaves and twigs, and Ziva was halfway to the feather when a hand wrapped around her arm and tugged her back.

"No!" The word fell out of her mouth as she skidded backwards, yanked to the gate, her hands splaying open with surprise, the feathers slipping from her grip. Almas's fingers dug into her flesh as he pulled her away, and the Milcham screeched as it dropped out of the trees right on top of the third feather. Ziva had enough time to see it spread its wings out wide before Almas pulled her around the corner of the gate.

Had the Milcham seen them?

Almas didn't pause. He kept running, Ziva in tow. The ground rumbled beneath them with the rhythmic pounding of heavy footsteps on the ground one after another, felt more than heard, under the bellowed demand, *"WHO?"*

Who?

So it didn't know who they were . . . but it did know they'd been there.

Almas ran them to an alley, and they vanished into it just as the sounds of the Milcham bursting out of the garden echoed up and down the street. The weighty flaps of its wings, the scrabbling of its claws on the stone, and the furious shrieks as it demanded to know who, who, who had come into its garden.

Ziva and Almas stopped running. If they kept out of sight, as long as they didn't make noise, hopefully they wouldn't draw the Milcham's attention. So they froze, pressed up against the wall, as the Milcham paced and muttered and swore it would find whoever was responsible.

The Milcham's shadow fell over the mouth of the alley, and Ziva's breath turned into ice in her lungs. She watched, eyes wide and terrified, as the Milcham's shadow grew and grew, and darkened, and soon swallowed up the whole alley. There was no escape. They were caught.

FORTY-FIVE

ZIVA AND ALMAS pressed against the wall, breathing as quietly as they could while the Milcham's shadow filled the alley the way water fills a trough, sloshing from front to back until it poured over the tops. The Milcham stalked on the other side of the alley's mouth, claws clacking on the stone.

And then its shadow lifted. It was moving away. Soon everything was quiet. The Milcham had, for all Ziva could tell, gone back into the garden.

Almas pulled on her arm again, attempting to retreat down the alley and find an exit on the other side, but Ziva resisted.

"No!" Ziva hissed, yanking her hand back and stopping. Almas stopped too, his face awash with confusion.

"Ziva, we have to go!" he said.

She pointed at the mouth of the alley, back toward the garden. "I need those feathers!"

Almas's mouth dropped open, and he gestured wildly at the garden's blue walls. "The Milcham is *in there!* It almost caught us!"

"We still have a chance," Ziva said, turning back. She made it three steps before Almas grabbed her again, pulling her away from the alley mouth while she flailed and smacked at him. "Let go of me, Almas!"

"I'm not going to let you do something that stupid just to get some magic feathers," Almas said. He was standing between her and the alley mouth, and now he put his arms up, blocking her way around him. She couldn't sneak around him, so she stood there, fists clenched so tight there wasn't blood in her hands, and she seethed.

"Magic feathers that will save Pesah!" Ziva snapped.

"And kill you in the process!"

Ziva spat, "So? Who cares? I'll die. *Fine.* Let me die for him. I'll get the feathers, throw them to you, and you get Pesah out of here."

"Why would you sacrifice yourself for him?" Almas asked, furious.

"Because he's better than I am," Ziva said.

Almas scoffed loudly. "How?"

"He's smarter." She said it so fast, Almas barely had time to take a breath. "He's brilliant. He could do so much good if he lived."

"And what else?" Almas asked, but didn't wait for her to answer. "He's so smart and that makes him better than you? More worthy of life?"

It was Ziva's turn to scoff now. "Of course it does."

"Why?"

"Because he could do so much—"

"So much good?" Almas interrupted. "Smart people aren't the only ones who can do good! Anyone can do good. Anyone can change the world. Not just the brilliant people."

Ziva squared her shoulders. "But the brilliant ones can do it better."

"Oh, can they?" Almas said. He put a hand on his chest. "I'm not smart. Not like Pesah is. But I can hear whispers of the future, Ziva. You don't think that puts me at an advantage? Hm? Knowing the future?"

She didn't answer him fast enough, so he continued.

"You!" He waved an open hand at her. "You might not be brilliant like Pesah, but when you sense any kind of injustice or unfairness, you're like a lioness on an antelope. I've watched you dig in your claws until you mauled a situation into equality and fairness for everyone involved. Pesah can't do that. And that's important."

"That's different," she said, somewhat resenting his description of her, especially the *mauled* part.

"It isn't!" Almas argued. "Being smart is not the best thing someone can be. Smart people aren't better than everyone else. Your life is worth living, and Pesah's is going to end soon, and you can't trade. Death doesn't work on trades."

Ziva clenched her fists, ground her teeth together, and searched her less-than-brilliant mind for a response to Almas. But there wasn't one that he'd accept. He was being *so stubborn*. Why did he even care if she traded her life for

Pesah's? If she could offer herself as a trade to the Angel of Death, she would absolutely . . .

. . . do that.

The Angel of Death was sitting outside the gates of Luz. He was there. He was waiting.

She left, turning her back on Almas and storming down the alley.

"Ziva." Almas grabbed her hand to stop her, and she whirled, yanking her hand away from his grip.

"Leave me alone!" she snapped, then hesitated, and shoved him in the chest for good measure. He staggered back a couple of steps, his face surprised and hurt.

Ziva turned again, charging away, and this time Almas didn't follow her. Good. There was no time to pay attention to him.

Ziva was going to bargain with the Angel of Death for her brother's life.

FORTY-SIX

THE CITY WAS DARK AND QUIET, the party having run its course and everyone having gone to bed. Evidence of the party was still there, but had been tucked away neatly for the next day's revelries.

Ziva arrived at the unguarded gates before she realized, and she stopped just inside. The brick road of the city ended abruptly on the other side of the gates, where the dusty cobbles of the worn road began. The moon was a slender curl above her, and the stars twinkled around it. A pleasant breeze rustled her hair as she stood at the threshold, bringing with it the scent of cinnamon and fresh bread.

The woman's body was gone.

The boy sat on the stone by the crossroads. The giant sword leaned against the stone, tip in the dirt.

He was looking right at her.

At the start of this whole journey, Ziva had told Pesah she'd poke out the Angel of Death's eyes. He had laughed, and so had she. Now, standing at the gate of Luz, staring down the Angel of Death himself, she realized what that promise had really meant. If she went out there to face him, she'd never come back. She'd be trading her life for her brother's.

And that was fine.

Pesah was a better person than she was, smarter, more noble, more giving—just more. No matter what Almas said about who was worth what.

She stepped outside the gate.

The cobbles were hard beneath her soles, and the pleasant scent vanished. The wind bit again, clawing across Ziva's face. The moon had lost its warm, silver glow and was instead harsh and flaying. She expected the boy on the stone to transform into the angel she knew he was, and descend upon her to gobble her up.

But he didn't move. He wasn't even paying attention to Ziva anymore. He was messing with a shallow box on his lap.

Ziva almost fled back into the city, but stopped. If she did that, they'd all be right back where they started. So she took another step, and another, and soon she was marching down the road toward the boy on the stone.

When she was ten paces from him, he looked up. Flaky filo dough crumbs clung to his lips and cheeks, and he held a perfectly square pastry in one hand.

He extended it to her. "Baklava?" he said through a full mouth.

Ziva narrowed her eyes. "I'm not falling for that."

He swallowed. "Falling for what?"

"I wouldn't take your baklava at the Asena camp, and now you're trying to kill me with it here," she said. "It's probably poisonous."

He looked down at the piece of baklava on his palm and shrugged. "Maybe." He looked back up at her. "I wouldn't know. Poison doesn't do anything to me."

"It'll do something to me," Ziva said, crossing her arms.

He nodded slowly. "Do you think you're destined to die by poisoned baklava?"

Ziva wasn't sure. His enormous sword seethed against the stone, as if angry it wasn't being used to flay her skin off right then and there. She said, "I don't know. Maybe you'll use that sword to kill me."

"Why do you think I kill people?" he said.

Ziva scoffed. "Because you're the *Angel of Death!*"

"So?"

"So, that's your whole job!" Ziva was absolutely incredulous. Did he think she was some kind of idiot?

"I guess," he said. "But I don't kill anyone. I mean, I don't cause the circumstances that lead to their death. I'm there at the end of the end, to free them from whatever pain they have." He glanced at the sword next to him and frowned. "I guess this is scary, huh? Well, I don't use it." He lifted a small, sticky hand. "Just this."

Ziva regarded his hand with a set mouth. He wouldn't use a sword to reap her into death. He'd use his tiny hand.

Chills skittered up Ziva's arms and neck, but she tried not to make them evident. She steeled her spine. "You can," she said. "But not yet."

She expected him to argue with her—to tell her it wasn't her place to say when she would die, or to get angry that she dared speak to him in such a way—but instead he smiled.

"You're right," he said. "Not yet."

Ziva swallowed hard. Her throat and mouth were dry, dry, dry, and her throat stuck to itself as she said, "Will you make a deal with me?"

He didn't respond for a long time. Then he held up the baklava again and said, "Are you going to eat this?"

"No," Ziva said.

"Are you sure?" he asked.

"Yes, I'm sure."

"It's really good."

"No!" she snapped, and he looked so sad and hurt that she sighed and said, "Do you swear it's not going to kill me?"

"Swear!" he said, so she took the baklava from him. It had been warmed by his hand, and when Ziva bit into it, she closed her eyes reflexively. Exquisitely honey-sweet and pistachio-crunchy and filo-crispy. Perfect.

The boy clapped his little hands. "See? I told you it's good."

Ziva mumbled, "You were right."

He patted the stone next to him, on the opposite side of the furious sword. "You can sit down if you want."

She hesitated, then sat, wiping her crumb-covered fingers on the stone. The boy reached into his pocket and pulled out a few skipping stones. He held out a hand full of pebbles to Ziva, and she wanted to ask him if he'd sent the ravens with their pebbles to Pesah in the wagon. Or if he had *been* the ravens.

She didn't ask, though. She just picked up a few of the stones and angled one at the calm surface of the pond, skipping it five times before it sank. The Angel of Death tossed one, and it skipped twice. They threw rocks in silence for a while.

"What deal?" he finally asked.

Ziva sank her last pebble. "My brother."

"Pesah," he said before she could.

She glared at him. She didn't like that he knew Pesah's name, although it wasn't surprising that he did.

"Yes," she said. "Pesah."

"Leprosy," the Angel of Death said to her. "It will follow humanity until its very end. You'll call it Hansen's disease later, after you've all made a cure for it."

Ziva was ready to tell him she didn't care what it would be called, but then blurted out with surprise, "There's a cure?"

"Almost!" He brightened. "Pesah's on the right track!"

Ziva was breathless then, heart pounding too fast for her lungs to keep up. "The salve from Geatland."

The boy shrugged. "Eh. The idea of it. The theory. The science. Salves won't ever help." He pointed at his open mouth. "You've got to eat it."

"He has to eat the salve?" Ziva asked, and the Angel laughed.

"It's not for you to know. And anyway, he's not dying of leprosy," he said. "Leprosy itself isn't fatal."

"But . . ." Ziva tried to understand what the angel was saying. Pesah wasn't dying of leprosy? How was that possible?

The Angel of Death handed her another few stones to skip. She took them idly, too shocked to turn them down. "Then what *is* he dying of?"

"Pneumonia," the boy said, resuming tossing stones. "It's, uh, an infection in his lungs. The leprosy made his body weak, and he can't heal from infections as well as other people. So he got an infection in his lungs, and pretty soon he's going to die because of it."

Ziva's mind just clicked, empty, over and over and over. His coughing. The rattling in his chest. Always breathing hard, like he'd just climbed a mountain. "Curing his leprosy wouldn't matter," she mumbled to herself.

The Angel of Death nodded. "It wouldn't matter no matter what," he said. "Rosh Hashanah started tonight. It's his time."

A sense of bitter smugness wrapped around Ziva as she said, "He's in there. You can't get him."

The Angel of Death smiled at her, then skipped a stone so well it hit the pond's opposite bank.

FORTY-SEUEN

HE WAS SO SMALL AND UNASSUMING, still peppered with baklava crumbs. Dressed like a regular boy with dark, dark hair and eyes like moss. Nothing angelic about him. No wings. No fire. Only two eyes and a voice like the small boy he resembled. But Ziva remembered the shadow he had cast: the roaring, winged creature with eyes that scorched his own shadow apart, and she shuddered.

"Are you going to throw those?" he asked, pointing to the stones in her hand.

Ziva tightened her fist around the pebbles. "Why do you do it?"

"Do what?"

"Kill people," she said.

He inhaled deeply. "I already said, I don't kill anyone. I just take them at their time."

Ziva kept her scowl to herself. Word games? That's what the Angel of Death was doing with her while she tried to bargain for her brother's life?

She threw one stone too hard, and it plunked into the dark water without a single skip. "This is what you do for all eternity. And you're happy with that?"

He stared at her, expressionless for a moment, and then threw his head back and laughed. He laughed loud and long, his small-boy giggles bouncing around the empty crossroads like frantic birdsong. Once he stopped, he said, "I've only done this for a few years."

Ziva scowled. "I'm not stupid."

"I don't think you are," he said, shifting so he could look directly at her. "My name is Azriel."

Ziva clapped her hands over her ears, the skipping stones clattering as they fell, expecting to feel the ripping pain of being torn apart at any moment. An angel's name! She'd never wanted to know that! She squeezed her eyes shut and waited for a sudden, explosive death, and—

Nothing.

She opened her eyes.

Azriel was watching her sideways.

"I didn't explode," she whispered.

"You did not," he agreed.

"You told me your name."

"I mean . . ." He lifted his shoulders up. "I sort of did. That's a version of it. You don't know the real one, because I don't want you to melt. Just like how right now, I don't look like my real self, because if I did, your eyes would pop! Anyway, Azriel." He pointed to himself.

"You already know my name," Ziva said.

He nodded. "Yes, I do. Ziva. And Pesah. And Almas. And Setareh, Sabriel, all of them. I know everyone's names, and I know, for the next year, who is going to die and when."

Her voice cracked when she said, "Pesah is a good person."

"Is he?" Azriel's heels continued to bounce against the stone. "He seems very kind. But sometimes it's hard to tell."

"So you know everyone's name and death, but not anything about them as people?" Ziva asked.

"No," he said. "Why would I need to know about them? It's not important."

Ziva bristled. "It's not important that Pesah is a good person, and smart, and could create a medicine to cure people?"

Azriel shook his head. "Nope."

"He could save people!"

"But he won't," Azriel said. Matter-of-fact.

"He will if you don't kill him," Ziva said.

Azriel didn't say anything. He stared at Luz, pondering it. His eyes were bright, reflecting the sliver of moonlight, and in the moon's reflection Ziva could see that, yes, he absolutely was an angel. Terrifying. Celestial. Burning, burning.

He blinked, and was a regular little boy again, covered with baklava crumbs. He turned to her and said, "We don't get to choose, you know."

Ziva didn't understand what he meant, and it was apparent on her face because he continued with, "Angels. We get assigned the Angel of Death position. We can't say no."

She blinked a few slow times. "You mean . . . you're—"

"I'm just a regular angel," he said. "Nothing special. And my time came to perform the Angel of Death role, so here I am. And it's not my favorite, but . . ." He leaned closer and whispered, "Baklava."

"Baklava?" Ziva asked.

He nodded. "Angels are ethereal. Baklava is corporeal. When I'm my regular self, I don't have a mouth. How am I supposed to eat baklava without a mouth?" He shook his head. "But as the Angel of Death, we get to be more corporeal. Any form we want. A lot of them choose to be big and flashy, but not me. I just want to be something with a mouth." He smacked his lips a couple of times and leaned back on his elbows. He stretched his head back, chin pointing to the sky. "It's like He knows delivering death is hard, so He makes it easier by letting us be something different while we do it."

Ziva didn't have to ask who Azriel was talking about.

He lifted a hand to point at the sky. "I've been there." He shifted his finger. "And there."

"To the stars?" she asked.

"Yes." He let his hand drop. "The benefits of being ethereal."

"What's better, stars or baklava?" Ziva asked.

"Baklava." He answered immediately. "No contest. Stars are lonely and loud and . . . majestic, I guess, but you can't eat them."

Ziva laughed in spite of herself, and then she remembered Pesah. In the city, he was still amputated and scarred and unable to walk, but he was alive. He was safe. He wouldn't die.

Azriel flopped back entirely on the stone, arms splayed out to either side. "Everyone dies, Ziva."

"I know." She shook her head. "But not Pesah. Not yet."

"What makes him special?" Azriel asked. "Tell me why I should spare him."

She glanced at him, heart tripping in her chest. Was he entertaining the possibility of a deal with her? If she convinced him, would he let Pesah live? She tried to think of what made him special, and she blurted out, "He's smart. You said so yourself. He's almost figured out a cure for his disease. He's kind. He always smiles, and he always assumes the best of people. He does mitzvot all the time. Constantly. It's annoying sometimes." She laughed. "He helps me do my own mitzvot. He . . ." Her throat felt tight. "He just deserves to keep living. He'll do so much good, if only he gets the chance."

Azriel listened silently, his arms still flopped out to either side. His poisoned sword hummed menacingly from its spot on the other side of the stone. He stared at the stars. After a stretch of silence, he said, "Pesah sounds wonderful."

"He is," Ziva said.

Azriel, still and flopped back, said, "Do you think Pesah would argue this passionately for his own life?"

Ziva knew for a fact that he would not, but she didn't say so. It didn't matter, though. Apparently, Azriel could hear her thoughts, because he said, "Why do you think he wouldn't argue for himself?"

"Because he's selfless!" Ziva said, but as the words left her mouth, she remembered Pesah's own statement when they arrived inside Luz, gasping and wheezing after the frantic escape from the little angel sitting before her:

I'm still sick, Ziva.

This place hasn't changed that.

Azriel was silent. Like he knew what Ziva had said was a lie, and he was waiting for her to correct herself.

"He wouldn't argue for himself because he thinks he's supposed to die," she said at last. "Because he's been sick for so long. People have told him he's going to die, and he's starting to believe them."

"But you don't believe them?"

Ziva opened her mouth to say no, but then . . .

The pale spot on her wrist.

She was going to die, too.

Azriel set his hand on hers. She didn't flinch away, even though she expected to fall over, dead. But that didn't happen. He just squeezed her fingers in a way that was entirely too grandmotherly for a young boy. Or an angel.

"Death is not a punishment," Azriel said. "The kindest and most noble people still pass into my darkness, not because of any crime or sin, but because they must." He swept his arm at the city twinkling in the night. "They all must. And they all will."

Ziva followed his gesture toward Luz. Death wasn't a punishment? Then why did it hurt so much? Why did it destroy everything around it, too? When Pesah died, it wouldn't just be Pesah who suffered. Ziva would be gouged by his loss, the loneliness, the ache of missing her brother, for the rest of her life.

Azriel patted Ziva's hand tenderly, and when he spoke, it was to offer a deal of his own.

FORTY-EIGHT

SHE RAN BACK INTO THE city, tears streaming down her face. She had known the Angel of Death was frightening, but she hadn't expected him to be so unimaginably cruel.

She turned a corner and nearly ran straight into Almas. They each put their hands up to ward off the other, then realized who they were fending off, and dropped their arms.

"Where've you been?" Almas asked, sighing. "We've been worried."

Ziva said, "I went to see him."

"See who?" Almas asked. "The Milcham again?"

"No," Ziva said. *"Him."*

Almas still looked confused, and then he looked horrified. "You didn't."

"I did."

"And you're still alive?" Almas asked. "How?"

Ziva looked around the streets. She felt like they were being listened to. "Let's talk about this with Pesah."

They were silent on the way back to the little house, and as soon as they walked in the door, Pesah looked up from his place on the sofa. "Ziva! Where did you go?"

She stopped at the door, letting it swing shut softly behind her, and she was suddenly ashamed of what she'd done. She'd tried to die in Pesah's place. He was going to be furious.

"I . . ." She looked down at the white spot on her arm. "I spoke to the Angel of Death."

Pesah just blinked at her. "You *what?*"

"I was . . ." She crossed the room so she could sit by him. Softly, she mumbled, "I was trying to bargain for your life."

"Bargain?" Pesah shouted. "Bargain with what?"

She sighed. "Just—"

"With your own life, Ziva!" Pesah said. "You think I don't know what you'd do?"

"So?" she spat. "So what if I offered myself to die? It's my life, Pesah. You can't tell me what to do with it."

Pesah let out a groan of frustration and slumped back against the sofa. Then he pointed a finger at her. "Well, you're not dead. You're here. So he must have rejected your offer."

"Yeah," Ziva said bitterly, remembering the angel's actual offer. "He did."

Pesah sighed. "I guess we're just trapped here, then."

Ziva was prepared to try to steal one of the Milcham's feathers still, but before she could advance to any thought beyond that, Almas said, "What'd the Angel of Death offer instead?"

Ziva glared at him. "Nothing."

Almas crossed his arms. "Yes, he did."

"Almas," Ziva said in a warning tone.

The sheyd ignored her. "You were bargaining with a *malach*," he said. "It's the same as bargaining with a sheyd. Or bargaining with a human. With anything. You offered him something, and he countered with something else. So what was the something else?"

Ziva tugged her sleeve down to cover up the lesion on her wrist. "It was something stupid. That I'm never going to accept. So it doesn't matter."

Then Pesah's bandaged hands were on her arm, pulling her sleeve up sharply, and Ziva wrenched away from him.

But it was too late.

"You have a spot," he said, voice thick. Pesah knew what that white spot meant. Of course he did. He had so many of them. "Ziva . . ."

"It doesn't matter!" Ziva said. "We're here, right? It won't ever get worse."

Pesah slumped against the couch again, bandaged hands going to the top of his forehead, elbows on his knees. Silent. Breathing hard. Then he sniffed back tears. "I should have told you no."

"No?" Ziva asked. "About what?"

"Staying with me," Pesah said. "I knew I could make you sick. I thought I knew, anyway. But then we had already spent all that time together—and you never got sick—and I thought . . ." His eyes glistened. "I thought it would be okay."

Ziva realized she was rubbing that spot on her wrist, and forced herself to stop. "It'll be okay."

He shook his head. "I was being so selfish."

"No, you weren't," Ziva said. "Selfish about what?"

Pesah squeezed his eyes shut. "I didn't want to be alone. But I should have been. To keep you safe. But you kept coming back and I should have told you no, but I always felt safer when you were around, but . . . but *you* weren't safe."

Ziva swallowed to steady her voice before she said, "It's fine. We're going to find a cure—"

"Stop," Pesah said softly, his hands sliding from his hair to cover his face. Behind his bandages, he mumbled, "I killed you."

Ziva put her hand on his shoulder. "Pesah, no, you—"

"Of course I did!" His hands were still covering his face, but Ziva knew he was crying. "I gave you the leprosy, just like . . . just like Baba and Uncle Sabriel said I would."

"Well." Ziva searched for something to assuage his guilt, to make him feel less bad about the white spot on her wrist. "The Angel of Death told me you're not dying from leprosy. He said it's not deadly."

Pesah sniffled under his hands. "Feels pretty deadly to me."

"He said it made you weak, and you got a lung infection," Ziva said softly, thinking of all the times she'd taken him out and around their gardens, wondering if one of those excursions had done it.

Pesah just breathed for a long time, and then he dropped his hands from his face and said, "What did the Angel of Death offer?"

Ziva stiffened her lip. "It doesn't matter."

"Ziva."

"It doesn't, because it was a stupid offer, and I'm not going to take it," she said.

Pesah just stared at her wordlessly, letting his celestial eyes do the pleading that his lips were unsuccessful at.

Ziva sighed heavily. The sigh turned into a scowl. "He said . . . Pesah, it was so cruel."

"Tell me."

Another sigh. "He said he'd take away my leprosy. Cure it." She paused. "If you died on Rosh Hashanah."

Pesah sat back on the couch, staring at the floor, but through the floor. Staring somewhere Ziva couldn't follow him. He stared without blinking until he started to cough. He pitched forward while Ziva patted his back.

Once the coughing was done, Pesah let his head hang. "This isn't living, Ziva."

"It's fine with me," Ziva said, hating the way the lie tasted.

Pesah laughed. "Not three hours ago you were saying the same thing. Railing against staying here. Insisting you could take the Milcham's feathers and free us all."

"I still could," Ziva muttered.

"I don't think it would matter," Pesah said. He looked at his bandaged hands, the stumps where his amputated fingers had been, then looked down at his twisted legs. "This is my life. It's been written that I die today. And if I'm going to die, at least I get to die saving my sister."

Ziva stood up, fists clenched at her sides. "No."

Pesah didn't stand. He just looked up at her and asked, "Why is it okay that you die for me, but not the other way around?"

"Because—" Ziva said, but stopped. Because he was good. Because he was smart. Because he was kind.

Because she loved him. And she didn't know how she'd live without him.

Pesah stood now, unsteady until he wrapped his arms around her. As he breathed against her, she could feel the rattle in his chest. A rattle that would be there forever.

He whispered, "You . . . would always help Sabriel change my bandages. And then when he was gone, you did them yourself. You'd make sure I had new books, even after the servants wouldn't bring them. You sat with me so I wouldn't be lonely. You took me out into the gardens after I couldn't walk. You've done so much for me since I got sick, Ziva. Now it's my turn to do something for you."

Ziva shook her head. "Pesah, no."

"Yes," he said, and he turned. On wobbling, twisted legs, he made his unsteady way to the door. Ziva stayed rooted by the couch, wanting to run after him and keep him upright. Make sure he didn't fall. But she couldn't help him walk to his death. She wouldn't.

He stopped at the door, gripping the frame. He looked back at her, eyes tearing up from the effort of walking. His bandages puffed out with every hard exhalation, and he lifted one arm up, hand held out to her like he was asking her to dance.

"Don't . . ." he said through heavy puffs of breath. "Don't make me . . . go alone."

Ziva's fisted hands relaxed.

Alone.

How many nights had she lain in the darkness of her room, filled with terror that Pesah had died alone?

Pesah kept his arm up as long as he had the strength, and then he let it drop. He sighed, turned, and began to hobble out the door. Two steps, and Ziva couldn't see him anymore.

She was alone. And so was he.

"Pesah," Ziva breathed as she ran across the room. On the other side of the door, he was slumped against the entry wall, breathing hard, struggling to continue, and she slid her arm under his, wrapping around his chest, and pulled him upright.

Neither of them said anything. They just walked slowly toward the city's gates, and Almas trailed behind, and the denizens of Luz emerged from their homes as the sky brightened.

FORTY-NINE

AZRIEL STOOD next to the stone again. The sword still leaned against it, tip in the dirt. The little angel didn't have any baklava this time.

Pesah leaned hard against Ziva at the city's open gates, the entirety of the city massed silently behind them. "That's him?"

She nodded, grateful for the overcast day so that none of them had to see Azriel's shadow.

Pesah attempted to stand up straighter. His blue eyes focused on the Angel of Death, who still stood a distance away. Azriel was waiting for them to come to him.

On Ziva's other side, Almas watched Azriel, too. He trembled, tense, uneasy. A half-sheyd in the presence of a *malach*.

"Help me walk," Pesah said.

He leaned forward, but Ziva dug her heels in.

Help him walk.

Help him walk to his death. Literally, to Death, who stood with his hands in his pockets by the crossroads stone. Death, who the night before had promised Ziva the secret of Pesah's cure, but in the same breath had told her that it was too late for her brother.

Pesah was dead the moment he'd walked into Luz.

He looked over at her, the bandages around his face whispering as they shifted against one another. "Ziva?"

She shook her head, unable to speak what she wanted to say: that Pesah could be happy inside Luz. He could live there forever. Ziva would get books for him somehow, get a laboratory somehow. If he stayed in Luz, he could create the cure for others. He could help—

"Ziva," he said. Softly. In the voice he would have used if he'd grown up to become a doctor. "Help me go."

When he leaned forward again, Ziva went, too.

The crowd behind them shifted wordlessly as they left the city.

As soon as Pesah stepped past the city's threshold, he collapsed. Ziva yelped as she caught him before he fell completely, clinging to keep him upright. Had Azriel killed Pesah from that distance? "Pesah!"

He coughed. The deep wetness rattled out of him. Between coughs, he managed to say, "Sorry."

Then Almas was on Pesah's other side, helping him up. He looped Pesah's arm over his shoulder and stood him up, assuming most of Pesah's weight. Ziva still clung to Pesah, but Almas was the one keeping him on his feet.

Pesah cleared his throat and said, "Thank you, Almas."

The half-sheyd nodded, shivering. "I'll get you there."

"Are you sure?" Pesah asked. "He's an angel."

"I'm not afraid of a stupid angel," Almas said, even though his voice was low and trembling. But he stepped forward anyway, holding Pesah up, and the three of them went to Death.

Pesah walked slowly, hobbling on his twisted feet. He breathed hard with the exertion, and with pain. Outside Luz, the city's magic was gone. Pesah was dying again.

Azriel waited by the stone. Small. Still. Watching them approach with his mossy, fathomless eyes.

When Ziva, Pesah, and Almas were halfway to him, he moved toward them.

Without the sword.

Gasps from the city behind them cut through the morning air to Ziva, and she very nearly spun around to yell at them to go back inside. Pesah's death was not a spectacle.

From Pesah's other side, Almas said, "Don't they have anything better to do?"

Pesah slowed. Not from fear. From exhaustion. And pain. Limping, but still trying. Ziva stopped him and Almas. "Rest."

Pesah laughed. "Okay." He leaned his head against her shoulder and breathed hard. "Who knew dying was so difficult?" He laughed again but it turned into a wheeze, clawing for breath.

Azriel approached as Ziva watched, Pesah's head on her shoulder. He was still so small, so harmless. More solemn than he had been that night, but not frightening. When he reached them, someone in the city screamed.

The fury in Ziva's chest broke. Like water boiling over. Pesah's head still sat on her shoulder, and that was the only thing keeping her from charging back to the city and screaming at them to go away, to stop watching, to have some respect. But then Azriel's eyes flashed, flaming and burning for a breath, and the gates of the city slammed shut.

The angel smiled at Ziva. "There."

The rage in Ziva blew out with every fast exhalation she made, and she finally was able to say, "Thank you."

Azriel shifted his gaze to Almas. As he did, the air around him darkened, sucking all the light into his skin. The day was cooler, almost chilly. Almas stood solid, holding onto Pesah, and he stared down the little *malach* with a set jaw, nostrils flaring.

Neither of them said anything, and then Azriel smiled. The air around him brightened. He nodded at Almas, and then he focused on Pesah. Pesah looked down, meeting the angel's gaze, and they were both quiet for a long time.

Pesah broke the silence: "It's an honor to meet you."

Azriel bowed his head a little. "I feel the same. Ziva told me all about you."

Pesah laughed, and the laugh turned into a violent coughing fit. Almas and Ziva almost dropped him. The cough was wet and racking, and by the time Pesah finished coughing his eyes were red and bloodshot.

"I'm sorry," Pesah said to the Angel of Death once his cough stopped, his voice congested and thick.

"It's okay," Azriel said. He held out his tiny, impossibly clean hand. "Are you ready?"

Pesah regarded Azriel's hand with eyes Ziva couldn't read. He had said he was ready. Did he still feel that way, standing beside Death itself? "Will it hurt?"

"No," Azriel said.

Pesah nodded. The three of them stared at Azriel's outstretched hand.

And in spite of Ziva's best efforts, she let out a sob.

Pesah turned his head to look at her.

Ziva shook her head, tears coursing down her face. She hadn't wanted to cry. She wanted his death to be peaceful. She could cry later. Not in front of him. She didn't want him to know how much pain she was in.

Death wouldn't hurt him, but Ziva's tears would.

She couldn't say anything past the sobs.

Pesah straightened as much as he could and hugged her tight, pressing his bandaged cheek against hers and whispering, "I love you, Ziva."

She clung to him, pulling him against her chest, intending to never let him go. If she hung onto Pesah tight enough,

Azriel couldn't possibly take him away from her. He couldn't.
He couldn't.

He couldn't.

Pesah held Ziva, and she let herself fall into him. It was only them. The *malach* and the sheyd were gone and the city was gone and the crossroads were gone, and it was only Ziva and Pesah embracing for the last time on the blue road, a road littered with apples on both sides. His arms around her were strong. Too strong. He was using all the strength he had left to give her the best hug she had ever gotten from him. Or from anyone.

And then his grip loosened.

He kissed her through his bandages.

He told her he loved her again.

He held her hand in one of his, and he leaned back.

The world returned around them. Almas and Azriel were there, standing apart, a temporary and silent peace between them. Pesah stretched his hand out, palm up, amputated fingers splayed open.

Azriel took Pesah's hand.

FIFTY

AND PESAH FELL.

Ziva fell with him.

Azriel vanished, winking away like smoke. His shadow sped across the ground, back to the crossroads stone, and the sword hissed away.

Almas had his hands on Ziva's shoulders, her arm, her back, but she didn't hear what he said, if anything. Pesah was on the ground, eyes shut, chest still. His hand was still warm in hers. Warm. Warm meant alive, didn't it?

Ziva said her brother's name.

He remained still.

She pulled him to herself, and soon his bandages were wet with her tears.

Almas sat by them both, and then he was gone. Ziva was alone.

Pesah cooled as she held him.

The white spot on her wrist was gone.

Then a raven came. It landed a little distance from them, holding something in its mouth. A plant with a bulb on one end and long, spearlike leaves on the other. The bird hopped to Ziva and placed the plant on Pesah's still chest, then cocked its head up at her. Down at him.

The raven set its beak on Pesah's face for a moment, and then it flew away.

Ziva watched it go, and then looked at what it had brought.

She knew the plant.

They had tons of it in Atil.

Garlic.

Spear-leek.

She left it there and stroked Pesah's face. She pulled the bandages off him so she could see all of his face. Her beautiful brother. Taken.

"It was garlic, Pesah," she whispered to him.

She thought that, maybe, he knew. That when he had died, he knew everything.

She looked at the crossroads stone, where Azriel had sat for so long, and wondered when she'd see him again, and if he would remember her.

Then Almas was back, driving the horses in Ziva's red wagon. He pulled up beside her and stood quietly for a few minutes, then said softly, "Ziva?"

She sniffed and wiped her wet face with her sleeve. "Almas."

"Are you okay?"

"No," she said. She stroked Pesah's face again, touched her brother's scarred lips. "But I think I will be. Some day."

Almas nodded. "Do you want to go home?"

Ziva did. She really did. "Are we allowed?" She looked back at the city. "We can just . . . go?"

"No one's stopping us," Almas said. "And if they try to, they'll have an angry half-sheyd to contend with."

Ziva wiped tears from her cheeks and nodded. "Let's go, then."

Almas helped her set Pesah in the back of the wagon, and the two of them went west.

To Atil.

Home.

And when Ziva got there, pulling the stolen wagon into her family's courtyard after almost two months gone, her mother and father ran out of the house and embraced her with a ferocity she never would have expected.

"Where have you *been*?" her father demanded in a choked voice.

"Pesah?" her mother asked through tears. Real tears. "Where's Pesah?"

Ziva looked at the wagon, driven by a sheyd and bearing her brother's body, and she took a deep breath . . .

. . . and told them everything.

FIFTY-ONE

A COUPLE MONTHS LATER, winter came to Atil. The city was blanketed in insulating white as Ziva performed the ritual she'd done since they'd brought Pesah home.

First, the kitchen, where Almas was apprenticed to the family's chef. He was covered with flour and powdered pistachio, and when he saw Ziva, he grinned and said, "You're late."

"Shut up," she said, but smiled when she said it. Almas wasn't the skinny, beaten-up teenager he'd been on their journey to Luz. Already, just a few weeks after Ziva's parents agreed to hire him in their kitchen, he had filled out. He was still tall, but now he was broad, and he had strong arms and hands from grinding and stirring and kneading. He still had the scar across his face, but Ziva had noticed the other boys at the synagogue asking him about it in reverent tones, amazed that he had lived through an injury like that.

None of them knew he was half-sheyd. They didn't need to.

He held out a little square of something to her, wrapped in paper, and she took it gently.

"Are you coming?" Ziva asked. Sometimes he couldn't, because there was some kind of pastry in the oven, and he needed to watch it.

But not today. He nodded. "Let me get my coat."

Outside, Ziva and Almas left footsteps in the snow that were soon filled in, making their way to the family's grave-yard, to the newest stone there. Pesah had joined their ancestors here, his gravestone obscured by snow clinging to its face. Ziva wiped the snow off so she could read her brother's name, and her heart ached as her eyes slid over it. Pesah had taken a piece of her heart with him when he died, and nothing had filled it yet.

But as Ziva unwrapped the paper from the baklava in her hand, the emptiness eased some. She blew the snow off the top of his gravestone, revealing the skipping stones she'd lined up there. In a clear spot between pebbles, she set the pastry down. Then she pulled another skipping stone out of her pocket, from the collection on Pesah's bookshelves. As she turned the stone over in her palm, she said to Almas, "Back when Pesah could walk, we'd go to the market, and he'd learn Greek from the merchants there. Just . . . walked up to them and started asking them how to say words, and they told him, and he learned it."

As she remembered the way he'd tripped over the Greek sounds—just for a few days, and then he'd mastered them—she pulled his face into her mind. His face after it was covered with bandages, and before. How he'd tried to teach her Greek, and how all he'd been able to get into her head was how to tell someone to go away. How he'd laughed about that, and used his new language skills to get them good prices on kourabiedes, delicious almond cookies, and they ate them as they wandered the city.

And for a moment, she felt like he was there, back inside her heart, filling up the emptiness with Greek and laughter and cookies. He only stayed for a moment. The hole in her heart was still there, but its edges were softer. Somehow.

Almas listened to her stories of Pesah wordlessly that day, like he did every day. Like he had baklava waiting for her every day to place on Pesah's gravestone. He glanced around furtively, then slipped his hand around Ziva's. He held her cold hand in his warm one and said, "I can make kourabiedes, you know. If you want."

Ziva nodded and smiled. "The best baker in Atil."

"Someday," Almas said.

"No, not someday," Ziva said. "Today. Right now. The best baker in Atil." She set the skipping stone on top of Pesah's gravestone, then leaned her head against Almas's chest for just a moment, sighed, and pulled away. She wiped the tear that was chilling the skin on her cheek, and she said, "I'd like some kourabiedes."

"Then you'll have some kourabiedes," Almas said. He held her hand tightly for another half a breath, then let go of it. He turned to head back to the kitchen, and Ziva grabbed his hand as they walked.

He looked down at her with wide eyes for a moment, then smiled. He breathed out a slow breath. And he held her hand tightly in his.

At the bottom of the hill, Ziva turned to look back at her brother's grave. A raven sat on top of it, straddling the baklava and stones carefully, and as Ziva looked, the bird snapped the treat up in its beak and flew away.

Ziva watched the raven fly off, and Almas said, "She stole Pesah's baklava."

"It's okay," Ziva said, smiling. "How could she resist? It's even better than stars."

FIFTY-TWO

At the beginning of this story, I told you that Ziva had set out to do three things: find a cure for her brother's illness, master a demon, and sway the Angel of Death, *malach ha-mavet*.

She did two of those things.

So, which two?

In those days, they used to end their stories like this: *And they lived long and happily, and died together on the same day.*

And, dear listener, that's exactly what happened.

Ziva and Almas got married, and Almas became a very successful baker. Ziva took her father's seat as a judge after he retired, where she pursued justice like a hound on a rabbit. They had many children, and when their ends came, they sat beside a pond together, skipping stones as they had for decades.

Of course, they had baklava.

Once, Ziva had wondered if, when the Angel of Death came for her, he would remember who she was and what she had done. And I can assure you that yes, yes indeed, the Angel of Death remembered her. Still remembers her.

How do I know this?

Because by the pond that night—a lovely, clear spring night—we skipped stones and ate baklava and talked as we had at the crossroad. She asked how I had been. Fine, I replied. Still *malach ha-mavet* for a few more centuries. How had she been? Well. Happy. With a hole in her heart, but one with smooth edges.

And when the baklava was done and the skipping stones were gone, I reached my hands out to each of them, and I said, "Are you ready?"

Almas nodded, but Ziva shook her head.

"Not yet," Ziva said with a soft smile. "I have a question for you first."

Almas coughed out a laugh.

"Oh, do you?" I said, lacing my fingers beneath my chin. "And what question is that?"

"You let us step out of Luz," Ziva said to me. "Even though people who go in can't come out. Why?"

"A fair question," I said to her. And she was right. I had given her the warning. She knew the price of entry into the city of life. I should have taken her and Almas when I took Pesah. But . . .

"I don't know," I admitted to her, sitting in the graveyard with baklava sweetening my tongue. "I suppose with all your litigating for Pesah's life, you convinced me to let you live yours."

"Ah," she said, squinting as she smiled. "I wish I'd known that sooner. It would have made for great bragging rights."

We laughed, and she looked up at the purple sky. "Which star is your favorite?"

And listener, I followed her gaze skyward. I knew which star, of course, right away. I slipped my hands around hers and Almas's.

"Come on," I said. "I'll show you."

THE END

AFTERWORD

There was one; there was no one.

I want you to get a map. Any map will do. Yes, even the map app on your phone. Now, find Greece. Aha! Hello, Greece. We're not investigating you today, I'm afraid. But you're a nice starting place.

Now, head east and north just a smidge, across the Aegean Sea, past Izmir, past Bursa, and up to Istanbul. Did you know that Istanbul was once called Constantinople? People from other places had different names for it, too. A city with a thousand names. But in the time we're going back to, the city of Istanbul was called Constantinople, and the empire it was the capital of was called Byzantium.

In the middle of the tenth century, a letter passed through Constantinople after weeks and weeks of being taken around and around. It was written by a Jewish man named Hasdai ibn Shaprut from Spain. He had heard a rumor from some Khorasani (Iranian) merchants that, far to the east, there existed an independent kingdom of Jews. Hasdai wrote a letter that he intended to reach the King of the Khazars, and off he sent it.

Well, that letter got lost. And found. And lost again. And then in Byzantium, authorities there stopped the letter from going further. And the letter began to go back west, back to Spain. But in Germany, another Jewish man, Isaac ben Eliazer, took the letter back east, through Germany, Hungary, Kievan Rus' (which you won't find on your map—it's gone now!) and finally, into the vast empire of Khazaria, into the hands of its king, Joseph.

Joseph wrote a letter back to Hasdai, but then the Khazar Empire vanished, defeated by Svyatoslav the Brave, the Grand Prince of Kievan Rus', only a few years later. And just like that . . . the Jewish Empire of Khazaria was gone.

But it survived in stories. First, in stories told by Arab historians, detailing how the Khazars were welcoming of any religion into their empire, and how the Khazars didn't practice Judaism like the other Jews these historians were familiar with. And then a Jewish historian penned a whole book entirely about Khazaria, called *The Kuzari*, where he has a hypothetical discussion with the Khazar king about his nation. But for the most part, Khazaria faded from memory, as just another one of the many transient nations that rose and fell on the Eurasian steppe.

So then, here is another story about Khazaria. Just my story. Just my imagining. And who knows? Maybe, twelve hundred years ago, a girl and her brother really did meet a demon and resist the Angel of Death on the steppe. And maybe they got the ending that the fairy tales promise:

They lived long and happily and died together on the same day.

GLOSSARY

GENERAL

bek: the khagan's warlord. The khagan and bek ruled the country side by side, and the bek was in charge of the army and had the power to kick out the khagan if he wasn't doing his job

bull's gall: the gallbladder of a bull; this little organ hangs out near the liver and produces *bile* to help digest fats

celestial: belonging or related to heaven; for colors, this indicates a sky-blue color

gangrene: when an infection gets so bad, the infected body part starts to die. This happens because the infection prevents blood and oxygen from getting to that body part. It smells really bad, and that body part will turn greenish-black. The name "gangrene" kind of sounds like it has "green" in it, but it's not talking about the color! It's from a Greek word, *gangraina*, which means "putrefaction (melting) of tissues." Yikes! It can be life-threatening, and the only way to save someone's life was to cut off the infected body part. Sometimes, that's *still* the only way to get rid of it, because the infection might be so bad that antibiotics don't even work

-joon: in Persian, a suffix added to a person's name, approximately meaning "my dear"; if you were to say "Sofiya-*joon*," you would mean "my dear Sofiya"

kaftan: a robe-like garment that Turkic tribes traditionally wore; they were usually knee- or calf-length and had long sleeves

kashrut: Jewish laws that ban eating certain foods (like a cow's butt!) and describe how some foods need to be prepared in specific ways. (Like not eating meat with dairy!) "Kashrut" and "kosher" are not the same thing. Kosher describes a food that complies with the laws of kashrut, and kashrut is the state of being kosher

kesil/kesilim: the Hebrew words for fooling spirit/fooling spirits; in this context, a specific type of sheyd

khagan: a Khazar king, who would traditionally rule the khaganate with a warlord, called a bek

khaganate: like a kingdom, but instead of being ruled by a king, it's ruled by a khagan

kippah: the traditional round head-covering worn by Jewish boys and men. (And women if they want to!) Also called a *yarmulke* (YA-ma-kah)

kohl: the original black eyeliner, worn by women, men, and even babies! Kohl was used from Israel to India to the Sahara. It was used to make someone's eyes more beautiful, but also to help reduce glare from the sun in the desert. Many people believed it would protect a person from the Evil Eye. It's still used in a lot of places to this day!

kourabeides: almond-flavored shortbread cookies from Greece that are very, very yummy. They're also eaten in other countries around the Middle East, and are sometimes called *qurabiya*

leprosy: currently called *Hansen's disease*, one of the earliest recorded human diseases, a bacterial infection of the skin and nerves. A lot of people think leprosy causes body parts to fall off, but that's not true! Leprosy means a person might not feel it when they get an injury, so they won't clean out a cut and the cut will get infected. Leprosy also makes the immune system not work as well, so that cut is more likely to get infected and maybe get gangrenous! And gangrene is such a bad infection, it often needs to be cut off someone so it can't spread. So that would happen to people with leprosy to save their lives. Leprosy used to be a permanent disease once someone contracted it, but nowadays can be cured with antibiotics!

lesions: sores; in Pesah's case, these sores are on his skin, but lesions can happen anywhere in the body, even inside someone's brain

malach/malachim: the Hebrew words for angel/angels

malach ha-mavet: the Hebrew name for the Angel of Death

mazzik/mazzikim: the Hebrew words for damager/damagers; in this context, a specific type of sheyd, but sometimes is a spirit separate from sheydim

mitzvah/mitzvot: commandment/commandments in Hebrew, and is any law or rule contained in the Torah

phthisis: the old Greek word for tuberculosis, pronounced *TIE-sis*. It literally meant "to waste away," because tuberculosis often meant a person couldn't eat, so they would lose a lot of weight. Tuberculosis also made people cough a lot, and they would eventually cough up blood. Tuberculosis used to be a death sentence, but in modern times, it can be cured with *a lot* of antibiotics!

Rosh Chodesh Elul: the first day of the Hebrew month of Elul

schematics: plans used to build engineering-related objects

selichot: penitent prayers, usually said in the period leading up to the High Holy Days (Rosh Hashanah and Yom Kippur)

sheyd/sheydim: the Hebrew words for demon/demons, although Jewish sheydim are much different than Christian demons

tavalodet mobarak: the Persian way to tell someone Happy Birthday!

Tengrism: the traditional shamanistic religion of Turkic tribes prior to Judaism, Islam, or Christianity. Genghis Khan was a Tengrist!

Zoroastrianism: one of the world's first monotheistic (only one god) religions, originating in Persia

NAMES *(in order of appearance)*

Ziva bat Leah (ZEE-va): means "radiance/light of God," and "daughter of Leah" in Hebrew

Pesah ben Mänäs (PEH-sa): "Pesah" is another name for the holiday "Passover," and during the time of Khazaria, it was common for Jewish parents to name their children after holidays. "Ben Mänäs" means "son of Mänäs" in Hebrew

Sabriel (SAHB-riy-EHL): a name of uncertain meaning, but which may mean "minister of God" or "hero of God." This is the name given to the Khazar khagan who led the empire's conversion to Judaism, who is sometimes also known as "Bulan Sabriel"

Reuven ben Kohen (roo-VEHN): means "behold, a son" and "son of a priest" in Hebrew

Setareh (SEH-tah-ray): means "star" or "fate" in Persian; Setareh may be the name that Esther was derived from

Mänäs (mah-NAHS): a name of uncertain meaning, which was recorded in ancient texts as a name used in the Khazar Empire. It is derived from a legendary Kyrgyz warrior and khan, Manas, who is said to have lived in what is now modern-day Kyrgyzstan over one thousand years ago

Benyamin (ben-yah-MEEN): means "son of the right hand" in Hebrew

Aharon (AH-ren): means "of the mountain" in Hebrew

Khatun (kha-TOON): a title of nobility in Old Turkic, meaning "lady" or even "queen"; recorded in ancient texts as a name used in the Khazar Empire

Khatir (KHA-tehr): means "idea" or "heart" in Arabic. It was recorded in ancient texts as a name used in the Khazar Empire

Parsbit (pars-BEET): a name of uncertain meaning. A woman named Parsbit or Prisbit lived in the 730s, and not much is known about her except that in many sources she's called "the mother of the khagan" and had immense power, even commanding a military force against Armenia

Rivka (RIV-kuh): means "to bind" in Hebrew

Shmuel (shmoo-EHL): means "God has heard" in Hebrew

Yitzhak (etz-KHAK): means "one who laughs/rejoices" in Hebrew

Leah (LAY-uh): means "delicate" or "weary" in Hebrew

Almas (ahl-MAAS): means "diamond" in Arabic and Persian

Chichäk (chee-CHAYK): means "flower" in Chuvash, a Turkic language from Chuvashiya in western Russia

Ekrem (eh-KREH-M): means "kind" or "generous" in Turkish

Azriel (ah-ZRiy-EHL): also spelled Azrael, means "God is my help" in Hebrew. Azriel is often the Angel of Death in Jewish and Muslim tradition

LOCATIONS

Atil: the capital of the Khazar Empire, located in present-day Astrakhan on the western side of the Caspian Sea

Bahr ul-Khazar: the Arabic word for the Khazar/Caspian Sea, a large body of water that sits north of Iran and south of Russia

Byzantium: an empire located in modern-day Turkey

Constantinople: the capital city of the Byzantine Empire. Today this city is called Istanbul

Geatland: one of the names for Sweden; also called Götaland

Khazaria: an ancient empire in approximately present-day Ukraine that legend says was an empire of Turkic Jews; the empire fell in 988 BCE after war with its neighbor, Kievan Rus'

Khorasan: an old name for a nation that spanned what is now parts of modern-day Iran, Afghanistan, Turkmenistan, Uzbekistan, Tajikistan, and Kyrgyzstan

Luz: a possible ancient name for the city Bethel, near Jerusalem. It's also a separate mythical city of eternal life where the Angel of Death can't enter

Persia: an ancient nation mostly located in modern-day Iran, but which once covered Iraq, Afghanistan, and other countries

Samkarsh: a city in southern Khazaria on the shore of the Black Sea

ACKNOWLEDGMENTS

WRITING A FIRST BOOK IS fun but tough.

Writing a second book is . . . impossible.

Writing a third book never happens. Sorry to tell you, but you didn't actually read a book just now.

Okay, fine! Just kidding! You did. I hope you liked it. It was kind of sad. Sorry about that. I used to work in the intensive care unit (ICU) at a hospital, and this book was sort of a way for me to sift through all those hard times for me, and for my patients, and for their families, and try to find something in it.

I also wrote this for my dad, a little bit. When I was writing that tough first book and dreaming of the impossible second, he was diagnosed with leukemia. He died before my first book was published. Actually, the official news of my book's publication happened on the one-year anniversary of his death.

It was a very emotionally complicated day. I destroyed a lot of tissues.

My dad and I didn't always get along, but he taught me a lot of things and he loved me regardless. There's a little bit of him in this book. I love you, Dad, and for the record, I didn't want to be right.

Weslie Turner, my first editor, was amazing and insightful and patient, and I'm so grateful to have worked with her on this book! Monica Perez assumed responsibility for this book and its feral gremlin author and has put tasteful and necessary finishing touches on the book that make it sparkle (the author does not yet sparkle, though we're working on it).

Rena Rossner, my unreasonably incredible agent, was (and still is!) this book's earliest and biggest cheerleader and the first person I made cry ugly tears with this story.

Safiya Zerrougui designed a breathtaking cover that continues to blow me away every time I look at it. She beautifully captured Ziva's determination, Pesah's wide-eyed assessment of the world, and Almas's reluctant isolation. She is a lovely person, too, and entertained all of my awkward fangirling of her art with grace!

Celeste Knudsen's gorgeous jacket design brings Safiya's beautiful art to life, and I'm so grateful for Celeste's work with this book as well as my others!

My daughter was my very first beta reader, and she left insightful and kind notes on the draft's pages that I intend to keep and cherish forever. If any middle grade writers need a beta reader who will leave you hand-drawn emojis in the margins of your books, let me know. I have a really good reference for you. Also, she asked me to let everyone know that she wants to meet someone who voiced a character in *Encanto*. Camilo is her preference, but she's not picky.

To Ally Malinenko, who read an early draft of this and gave me incredible feedback on Pesah's story, thank you! You kick butt, and so do your books!

There are a lot of people out there who didn't read this book in particular, but who are always around when I need to talk, vent, or be weird. They've read other books or chapters, or they've listened and given advice while I planned a new story. You know who you are, and I hope you know how essential you are to me (especially now, after I just told you).

Last but absolutely not least, thank *you*, dear reader. I'm so glad you joined me for my third story, and I hope you'll join me for more.

Sofiya Pasternack

MORE BOOKS BY SOFIYA PASTERNACK:

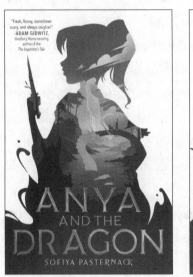